Addicted to him Part 3
By:
Linette King

Acknowledgements

First and foremost I want to thank God who is the head of my life and household. Without you I am nothing!

To my children: Aaliyah, Alannah and Jaye! You guys are my life and no matter where life takes you, I'll always have your back! I love you!

To my family: I love you all! Feels like my acknowledgement section is getting smaller and smaller. lol! Thanks!

To my friends: Jasmine, Trinisha, and Ashleigh thank you guys for not switching up on me! Yall are still as crazy as ever but I love it. Ya'll are stuck with me and if you ever try to stop being my friend I'm going to be at your door with a pistol!

To my readers: Thank you so much for continuing to read! Don't forget to leave a review! Love you all!!

Mississippi Gulf Coast! I'm going to make it and they will know more positive things about people from The Coast!

Big Shout out to my brother from another mother, B2Smoove! (BHG)! Man Brandon know I'm crazy and all he do is laugh at me! He's going to be doing big things on the music tip though. Check him out: instagram.com/bhg_bmiles23 twitter.com/bhg_bmiles23 facebook.com/bmiles23

Another shoutout to the big homie Rell! That man is something else with his caking self! Big Homie be jamming forreal though! Check him out http://m.datpiff.com/search/yung%20hr

Lastly but definitely not least my boy Darius Pierce! I've never in my life talked to a man my age that has a mindset like him. He brings nothing but positive energy and he's really trying to change the way people view our community. I admire him as a man and I admire his plan. I believe that everything he has set out to accomplish will happen because he won't have it any other way. He already has this annual health awareness rally that he has in a different city of the coast each year and next will be his radio talk show. For great health tips, business tips and inspiration find him on Facebook. https://www.facebook.com/BIGDOGENT228?fref=ts

Prologue
Tamia

When Steve threw me in the back of the cab, I didn't even fight to get out. I just laid back thinking of the days of my life when everything was carefree. All the way back when my mom was still alive and it was us against the world. Back when grades weren't an issue and boys weren't a thought. I would give anything to go back to those days and get out of my current situation.

"What the fuck?" Steve said out loud, snapping me out of my thoughts. I sat up and looked out the window and saw Deuce, Brandon, and Candy following closely behind us. I smiled on the inside because I knew they were going to save me. It's beginning to look like a pattern with Brandon saving me and Rashard being M.I.

Steve swerved hard, sending me flying into the door. I sat upright and put my seatbelt on. He continued to drive crazy trying to lose them, but I knew they would save me. I knew from the look on Candy's face back at the house that she was going to come find me. I looked out the back window again when Steve turned off. I started to panic when Deuce kept driving.

"Don't look so scared Tamia. I'm going to have fun with you," Steve said, looking at me through the rearview mirror before parking the cab.

"Suck a dick!" I said back to him, causing him to frown, probably from the memory of what happened to his. "Do you have a dick Steve? I know we did a number on you. Did they cut it off to save your life?" I asked, fucking with him. He reached back and stabbed me in the leg with an antenna, causing me to scream out in pain. The pain subsided as I stared at the antenna in my leg and started laughing. Steve looked at me like I was crazy. "I'm going to kill you but don't worry, it will be quick." I said and Steve pulled off.

When I looked back, I saw Deuce found us and was now back behind us. "1, 2, they're coming for you. 3, 4, you shouldn't have come for more. 5, 6, Steve's got no dick!" I sang like I was singing the Freddie Kruger song. Steve didn't respond. Instead, he pushed the antenna deeper. I laughed loudly because I knew I was going to kill him. POW! A gunshot sounded, making me look back to see my knight hanging out the window with a gun. We swerved slightly but Steve was able to gain control of the vehicle.

I sat back, waiting for them to shoot out another tire but they didn't. BOOM! A car hit us from the side and we flipped about four times. My seatbelt broke after we landed upside down and I fell on my head. I grabbed the antenna and snatched it from my leg and stabbed Steve in his stomach with it. Candy came out of nowhere, snatching me out the car and pulling me towards the truck. "Do you have a gun?" I asked and she looked at me sideways. "I need to kill him or he will come back," I explained.

She waved Brandon over because Deuce ran off to the car that hit us. "She need your gun," Candy said to Brandon. He grabbed my other arm and lifted me higher. The smell of his cologne was making me horny. I know sex should be the last thing on my mind but I hadn't had actual sex since Amere over four years ago!

We got to the car just in time for Steve to be trying to wiggle his way out the window. I pulled away from Candy and Brandon, so I could do this alone. "Hey Steve!" I said, catching his attention. "You should have left me alone," I said before squeezing the trigger. I was aiming for his head but when the gun jerked, it caused me to hit his neck. I watched his eyes close before walking closer to check his pulse. Yep! He's as dead as a door knob, I thought to myself smiling before falling backwards.

Brandon scooped me up and carried me to the truck. "You smell so good," I said, shocking myself. He smiled and sat me in the backseat. When I looked to my right, I saw Rashard and his legs were bleeding something serious. "Are you ok?" I asked him because he didn't look so good.

"You asking me like you ok," he said before passing out. I pulled my shirt over my head and ripped it in half. I tied both pieces *around his legs above the wounds to slow the bleeding down. I reached over and checked his pulse and it was barely detectable. He was losing way too much blood.*

I looked up at Deuce, who was glancing back occasionally. When our eyes connected, he nodded his head. Several minutes later, we pulled up to Doc's house and went through all the same shit we went through last time. We all took our shoes off, the bitches were still rude, and his wife was still doing her damn make-up.

"You ready?" Doc asked me. I stood to my feet and headed into the examination room. I knew I was fine but it was Rashard that I was worried about.

"How is he?" I asked Doc as he gave me a tetanus shot for my leg wound.

"He lost a lot of blood and has slipped into a coma. I have my people bringing blood over to give him a blood transfusion and after that, of course, you know it's up to him," Doc said, cleaning my face.

After I was done, we all left and went back to my apartment. Candy and I stayed in the car while Deuce and Brandon loaded a few boxes in the very back. Instead of staying at Candy's house that night, we all stayed over at Deuce's house.

Lisa

I'll never understand how this happened. My baby didn't survive long enough for the doctor to find her any blood. I've been crying ever since it happened. I didn't leave out the room for anything! I prayed and prayed and prayed but my prayers weren't answered! Now my baby is gone. My precious Amiria is gone and everyone involved will pay.

I walked out of the hospital making a call to Andre. "What's up baby?" he answered the phone.

"My baby is dead, and now Tamia and everyone she loves must die," I said.

"I've been waiting on you. I'm in the parking lot."

"Alright, I'm on my way out," I said, about to hang up when he called my name. "Yes?" I asked.

"I got some people out here with me who's ready to bring it," he said, disconnecting the call.

"Everything's going to be ok," the nurse said that had been with me. I completely ignored her as I made my way outside, looking for Andre. When I spotted him, he was standing around a group of people next to a van.

"Hey everybody," I said with a light smile.

"I'm sorry for your loss babe," Andre said, walking up to me before giving me a hug. "Let me introduce you to everybody. Everybody here has some type of beef with Tamia, Rashard, and Armani, so we're going to take them out, together. This is my boy Twan, Tiffany, Michelle, and Bo. Twan is tired of being under Rashard while he play us like we don't know he's running shit. Tiffany is here because her cousin Michelle is here. Michelle is tired of Rashard hurting her and she wants to kill Tamia. Bo is Rashard's brother and he has always hated him," he said, nodding towards the people leaning against the van.

I looked over at the small woman that wore baggy pants and a large jacket with the hood tied securely around her head. "Who is that?" I asked.

"That's Daphney. Tamia and Armani ruined her life when they tried to kill the love of her life. She thought he was dead and got addicted to drugs. When he got better, he came to find her and got her clean before they both came looking for Tamia and Armani. They found Armani first and she's been torturing her everyday but they don't have her anymore. She just wants to hurt them how they hurt her," he explained.

"Oh my gosh. How do you know them?" I asked Daphney.

"I'm Armani's mother," she said, causing my jaw to drop because I had no idea Armani even had a damn mother, and we're all from the same place. I looked over at Andre, who was smiling at me.

"The man they tried to kill is my uncle I was telling you about," Andre said to me.

"So it's set. We're killing them all?" I asked. Everyone nodded their heads.

Tamia

It's been weird going to visit Rashard every day. It's been almost three weeks since he slipped into a coma and he hasn't woken up yet. I met his sister, Myra, through Candy and she had been going to the school picking up his assignments. Luckily, he took finals before this happened. Anyway, Myra gives his assignments to me and once I complete them, I turn them in. Our graduation is literally right around the corner and I'm afraid he won't be able to walk across the stage. I go sit with him at Doc's house every chance I get. I only stayed off from work a week before I returned with lifting restrictions. I was still able to get vitals on patients; I just wasn't able to assist them.

In between work and Brandon, yes I said Brandon, it's not much time left for Rashard. I like Rashard but we hadn't put any titles on anything before this happened and I was more than likely going to pull away anyway. Brandon has been my savior! I sat down at Candy's house with her and told her how I felt. It was like every time I needed to be saved, Brandon was the one to save me. It shouldn't have been Brandon; it should have been Rashard. That's why when he asked me to go out on a date with him, I agreed.

We've been kicking it really hard these past two weeks and I'm really loving the type of guy that he is. He's extremely courteous. He opens doors and pulls out chairs. He calls me daily to tell me good morning and to see how my day went and I love the attention. We have been out on ten dates in two weeks. We haven't had sex and I'm honestly passed ready to get this box beat up. It's been years! Nobody has been in this since Amere. I'm well aware that I can sleep with anyone I want but that's not the kind of person I am. I have a lot going for myself and I don't want to get hurt.

For me, sex is an emotional connection. I can't have sex with someone I'm not emotionally attached to. I'll never understand how Armani can just give it to any and every man that will pay for it. Well, she's not that loose but she's been screwing at least four people at once. She kept them in rotation, making sure she was always available to them all. That's a job within itself. I haven't seen her at all since she's been free from Steve and that's fine with me. I'm just glad she's ok.

"Have you started inviting people yet?" Candy asked me, snapping me out of my thoughts. I had been staying with her and everything was perfect. We get along perfectly like siblings, which in all honesty, really isn't perfect.

"I don't have anyone to invite," I stated. I looked up at her as her smile faded away.

"Girl, if you don't smile, I'm going to kick yo yellow ass! I didn't do this for anyone else. This graduation is for me. It's ok," I said, giving her a reassuring smile.

"What about Armani?" she asked with a serious expression on her face. We hadn't talked about her at all after I gave her the rundown of our friendship and ended with how I found out she had been sleeping with Amere.

Speaking of Amere, he made it through and as soon as his wounds heal, he'll go through physical therapy. As far as his daughter, who wasn't really his daughter, she didn't make it. I wanted to reach out to Lisa and give her my condolences but I didn't want her to think I was trying to be funny, so I left well enough alone. A simple prayer request that God gives her strength to deal with this was all I needed to do.

"I have no idea how to get in touch with Armani," I said, looking at the TV. I heard Candy suck her teeth before walking out of the living room. I always think it's funny how Candy sucks her teeth and walks away when she has an attitude. Normally, she would say whatever she wanted to say then walk off before you can respond. What she didn't know was that when she does that to me, I will follow her to the ends of the earth to get the last word. *Ding* My text message tone going off caught my attention.

Brandon: wyd baby

Tamia: well I was talkin to Candy but she walked off lol

Brandon: get dressed im comin to get u

Tamia: is that question???

Brandon: Did you see a question mark?

Tamia: ugh I wasn't planning on doing nething today

Brandon: i didn ask wat ur plans were. c u n 15

I didn't bother responding because he's going to come anyway. When we first started talking, his aggressive attitude was a major turn on. Sometimes it still is but when I don't really want to be bothered and he does it, it's aggravating. Candy warned me about him and I didn't listen. She told me it was only going to get worse but it hasn't. I always make sure I tell him we're just friends, so it's not like I'm leading him on or anything. For some reason, I'm holding on to the little hope I have that Rashard will get better and we will be together. That's just wishful thinking though.

I like Brandon but there's just something eerie about him. He has this gloomy presence about him when we aren't talking. It's hard to describe but I'll try. Have you ever been around someone and whether you're, talking, laughing or being quiet, it's peaceful? Well, with Brandon, as long as we're laughing or talking, it's fine. When we aren't talking, the silence is deadly. That's why I'm never alone with him unless we're in the car. We have been on plenty of dates but it's never a chill at his place type of thing.

"Hey Candy!" I yelled, walking to her room. When I got to the door, she signaled for me to give her a moment with her finger. I could see the smile on her face and she was shaking her leg.

"Ok, we will be right over," she said before she hung the phone up. She turned to face me with a smile on her face. "Bitch, what the hell you smiling for?" she asked me. I didn't realize I was smiling until she said that.

"I don't know. Why we happy?" I asked, laughing.

"Because Rashard is awake!" she said, jumping up and down. My jaw hit the floor.

"Where you goin?" Candy yelled at my back because I ran out of her room.

"I have to get dressed, so we can go!" I yelled over my shoulder. I rummaged through my clothes until I found some dark blue jean skinny legs. I rolled the bottom of them up to my calf to bring attention to the brown sandals that I wore wrapped around my ankles. I threw on a bright yellow cropped top shirt that read "I'm Yours" across my small breasts. I grabbed a brown belt to match the shoes and I was good to go. I hadn't had my hair done since Deuce's birthday party, so I just threw it up in a messy bun and let a few curly strands dangle around my face.

"Ok, I'm ready," I said, walking in the living room to an already dressed Candy. She wore a long flowing multicolored maxi dress. Her thong style sandals were also multicolored. She wore silver accessories with her hair in a tight ponytail.

"You said that like it took you five minutes when I've been sitting in here for ten," she said as she rolled her eyes playfully at me.

"Oh hush, let's go!" I exclaimed as walked swiftly to the front door.

I swung the door open and ran directly into Brandon. I was so excited about Rashard being awake that I wasn't paying any attention to where I was going. When I bumped into him, he dropped his phone, which is probably why we ran into each other. "I'm sorry," I said, reaching down to pick the pieces to his phone up. He grabbed me and pulled me out of reach of his phone and picked it up himself. A frown graced his handsome face.

"You good," he said as he put the pieces back together.

Candy walked out of the house, reminding me that Rashard is awake. I stood there looking between Candy and Brandon. She had a smirk on her face and he hadn't looked up yet. "Hey Brandon, I can't go with you," I said nervously. I have no idea why I'm nervous but I am. In the two weeks, I've never had to tell him no and stick with it. He's always been able to get me to change my mind or rearrange my plans. The only thing he never tried to interfere with was work and that's because I let him know upfront that it was very important to me. Trying to stop me from getting the hours could mess with me graduating on time and as far as I've come, I was not about to let a man come between me and success.

"The fuck you mean you can't come?" he asked, then looked over at Candy.

"Hey, don't look at me," she said with her hands up. "I'll be in my truck," she said to me as she walked passed me to get her truck. "Rashard is awake. We're going to see him," I explained as I fiddled with my fingernails.

"Oh ok. Well, call me later," he said and walked away. I was shocked that it went so well but glad it did.

Candy

Living with Tamia has been peachy but I really wish she had listened to me and not got involved with Brandon. Sure, he's handsome and charming and don't get me started on his eyes, but that's like the calm before the storm. I'm a friend to them both so I couldn't exactly indulge too much, but I let her know he's crazy and suggested that she not talk to him. I've known Brandon awhile and Deuce has known him even longer, and even he asked me why I hook that up. Truth be told, their little match up had nothing to do with me. I'm so glad Rashard is ready to get up because I need him to step up for Tamia and take her away from Brandon.

When I got the call to come to Doc's house, I was overjoyed with emotions because I've been witnessing the stress him being out of pocket has caused Tamia. I really think she's been through enough already but now she's starting to make dumb choices. Most girls get mad when they find out later on down the line that the nigga they fucking with is crazy, but I told her as soon as I saw she was interested. I noticed she fought the attraction for a good week after the accident but I wish she would have held out a little longer. I tried telling Rashard to get it together but being a friend to Tamia, I couldn't tell him why.

Rashard has been having this ongoing issue that he's been trying to fix but I'm going to let him tell you about that.

When I walked out of the house behind Tamia and saw Brandon, I shook my head. Nigga had the nerve to look at me like I'm the reason she's cancelling a, probably, unplanned date. I just went ahead to my truck and called Deuce.

"What's up?" he answered. I could barely hear him over the music but he's always in a noisy environment.

"Can you turn that down for a minute?" I asked with my face screwed up. We finally made this thing official but now we're taking things one day at a time because neither one of us are used to being in a relationship.

"Lemme walk outta here," he said. I crank my truck up as I waited for him to leave out of the noisy room he was in. "What you got going?" he asked, once he was outside.

"Rashard is ready," I said.

"Finally? Took his ass long enough." he said with this nonchalant attitude. Deuce is the only one, other than myself, that Rashard trusts and I think it's because Rashard knows I trust Deuce.

"Tell me about it," I said, as I watched Tamia and Brandon have a quick exchange.

"Look, I gotta go but I need you to keep a handle on Brandon for me; you know how it gets," I said quickly.

"That man grown as fuck," Deuce said.

"Yea, but he's crazy too and this my girl," I said.

"And I'm yo nigga and he my cousin! Leave that shit between them. Shit, you did yo part, now mind yo business. Call me later," he said and hung the phone up in my ear. I pulled the phone away from ear and stared at the phone in disbelief. I let out a deep frustrated breath as I watched Tamia walk to the truck.

"That was easy," she said, as she snapped her seatbelt on.

"Too easy," I replied, as I looked behind me. Brandon was taking his time getting in his all black Charger and letting me out. Shit, we couldn't go anywhere until he moved from behind us but it looked like he was playing on his phone. "What the fuck?" I asked and gestured for Tamia to look back. When she looked at what I was looking at, she rolled her eyes and sat down.

I laid on the horn to get his attention. It must have pissed him off because he backed his car up and burned rubber. I peeled off in the opposite direction. *I hope like hell Rashard knows what he's doing*, I thought to myself as I shook my head.

"What's wrong Candy?" Tamia asked. I glanced over at her as she rotated her body, so she could face me. I couldn't tell her what I was I thinking.

"It sucks being caught in the middle," is what I wanted to say. "Deuce's childish ass," is what I actually said.

"What he do?" she asked, but I just shook my head and turned the music up.

Funny thing is, the song that started playing is perfect for Rashard's current predicament. I bobbed my head to *Smooth Blues Song* by Carl Mims, as he sang about being caught up in a two-way love affair. I glanced over at Tamia and she had tears in her eyes. I thought about the lyrics of the song and as fucked up as it is, it's perfect for her too.

Being that I'm friends with them all, it's not much I can do at this moment but change the station. "I never fucked Wayne. I never fucked Drake," Nicki Minaj said, which wasn't any better since Tamia hadn't fucked Rashard or Brandon. The song made with Drake and Wayne called *Only* blared through the speakers.

Fuck it, this my song. Tamia gonna have to tough it out, I thought myself as I continued to drive. I glanced over at her and she still had tears welled up in her eyes but she didn't let them fall. I'm not going to push the issue because I honestly just don't feel like I can hold anymore secrets. Hell, lately, I've been wanting to just quit talking to all these mufuckers because they're all forcing me to keep secrets that I didn't ask to hold.

A few minutes later, I was pulling up to Doc's house. I took a deep breath and looked over at Tamia. She was so excited that she didn't wait for me to get out before she was walking to the door. "God, please don't let this go left," I said out loud. I shook my head and followed her to the door.

Rashard

I sat in Doc's living room a nervous fucking wreck after I told Candy that I was finally ready to face the music. Chardae is indeed pregnant and she's far enough along to know what she's having. It's a boy. Wait, let me take you back so you won't be confused.

The day of the accident, I passed out on my way to Doc's house. Well, we were in the operating room alone when I woke up. I gave Doc a quick rundown on the bullshit that was happening in my life and he agreed to help me out. I gave him $6,000 to make Tamia think I was in a coma while I got things straightened out with Chardae. Call it what you want but I'm not trying to lose Tamia and I'm going to be a father to my child. Well, if he's mines.

Anyway, Doc has it set up to where she has to call before she comes. After she calls him, he calls me, and I leave Chardae and come back to Doc's house where he puts me under until Tamia leaves. Now, Candy knows what's been going on and, believe me, she curses me out every damn chance she gets, but I know Candy will never betray me.

Before you go to turning your nose up at me for making Tamia think I've been in a coma, try thinking about it from my side of things. I've just really started to get close to Tamia and I know the possibility of me having a child will ruin that. Tamia deserves a life that only I can provide for her. All I want to do is make her fall in love with me before Chardae has the baby. That way, if the baby is mine, she won't want to leave me and if it isn't, then we won't have a problem at all. Either way, I'm not telling her about Chardae possibly being pregnant with my child. Hell, she's not going to know a thing about a baby until after the results and that's only if the baby is mine.

"I think you should wait in the bed she's been visiting you in," Doc suggested.

"Why?" I asked with a confused look on my face.

"A person that's been in a coma for three weeks doesn't just get up and walk away, Shard. Tamia is smart as fuck and she will know something is off," Doc explained.

"Iight," I said, as I stood to my feet. I got up to follow him to the back, just as his front door was opening. "Fuck!" I said softly to myself.

"Tamia, wait!" I heard Candy yell. I peeked slightly around the wall and noticed Tamia had her back to me. I hauled ass through Doc's house and hopped on the cot he had been having me lay in, in his late wife's room. Well, I don't really know if I should say late wife since her stuffed corpse is still here at the vanity station. I glanced over at her and wondered what he do to keep her hair up. Shit's weird.

I could feel my phone vibrating in my pocket but I could hear them walking this way. I quickly pulled out my phone and shut it completely off without checking the message first. I slid it back into my pocket just as Tamia turned the corner with tears in her eyes. "Cut all that out baby, I'm good. I made it," I said as I smiled at her. I didn't miss the look Candy gave me as she stood there with her arms folded.

"Oh my gosh, I'm so happy you're ok! Listen, you don't have to worry about school because Myra's been getting your assignments and I've been doing the work. Graduation is still set, so we just have to get your strength up," she said all in one breath. I nodded my head at her and gestured for her to get me a cup of water. She walked off immediately and came back with a cup of water for me. She helped me sit up and drink the water from the cup. "Don't try to drink it too fast," Tamia said. I looked over at Candy, who was rolling her eyes up in her head.

"What's up sis?" I asked because she wasn't acting like a nigga just woke up out a coma. She was about to fuck everything up with her attitude.

"Nothing much. You don't act like you been a coma," she said sarcastically. I almost choked on my spit when she let that shit fly out her mouth. I see now that she really is pissed about how I handled the shit, so I'm not going to hold that against her.

I looked at Tamia, who had a weird expression on her face, but she didn't say anything. "Can ya mans get a hug or something damn?" I asked in a joking manner. I needed to lighten the mood because I could see the wheels turning in Tamia's head after Candy's little comment. She hesitated, looked at Candy, then reached her arms around my neck to hug me. She smelled so good and I closed my eyes to take in her scent.

"Have you tried getting up?" Tamia asked with her phone in her hand. I watched her suspiciously scroll through her phone like I ain't just wake up from a coma.

"The fuck you doing?" I asked with a frown on my face. She looked nervous as she locked her phone and slid in her purse.

"Have you tried getting up?" she asked, completely ignoring my question.

"No, now who the fuck you been talking to?" I asked. I was so pissed off that she was talking to somebody else. I shot daggers at Candy for not telling me what the fuck Tamia had been doing because I know she knows. Candy rolled her eyes at me, so I refocused my attention on Tamia as I waited for her to answer.

"Listen Rashard," she began.

"Don't listen Rashard me! You couldn't wait?" I asked seriously. How the fuck can I trust a bitch that couldn't wait a few weeks for a nigga to wake up out of a coma before she started fucking with another nigga? Ok, granted I wasn't really in a coma, but she didn't fucking know that! Tamia stood next to the bed with a shocked expression on her face.

"Look, you need to calm down," she said, as she placed her hand on mines softly. I snatched my hand away from her as I stared into her eyes.

"Did you fuck him?" I asked. Her once shocked expression turned into one of anger.

"Fuck you! I'm glad you're ok but don't contact me again, EVER!" she snapped and left out of the room.

I looked over at Candy, just as she begun to shake her head at me. "What?!" I snapped at Candy.

"I thought you were ready to tell the truth," she said calmly and walked off. I know they rode together, so I know she's going to make sure she's ok and take her home.

"Man fuck!" I screamed as Doc came trotting into the room.

"Some reunion," he said, as he grabbed a brush off the dresser and started brushing his wife's hair. I shook my head as I climbed off the bed and powered my phone back on.

I checked my messages and saw that Chardae texted me asking for some butter pecan ice cream. I grabbed my keys and headed for the door to get what she wanted. Since Tamia pissed me off, I'm going to do exactly what she want me to do and leave her the fuck alone! I'm not about to chase her; hell, her name ain't check and that's the only thing I'll chase.

I pulled up to the grocery store and bumped into my boy, Twan. "What up bro?" I asked, as I dapped him up.

"Shit, chillin man. Where the hell you been?" he asked, as he turned around to walk in the store with me.

"Here and there my nigga," I answered. Anybody that knows me knows I don't deliver details about my whereabouts to any damn body, so I don't know why he even asked.

"Iain see ya in Dead Man's Zone lately," he pried.

"I'm bout to let this shit go bro," I said, as I grabbed the ice cream and headed to the checkout counter.

"Oh yeah?" he asked with excitement evident in his voice. I nodded my head and he walked off with his phone in his hand.

Must have had a bitch hitting him up, I thought to myself. Between him and Dre, I don't know which one let a bitch distract them more.

I hopped in my car and drove to Chardae's new house. I had to move her out the damn hood because I didn't want my son growing up in the hood and leading the life I'd led. Her new house is uptown in a really nice neighborhood. It's only about an hour away from the house I bought for Tamia and I to move into.

I pulled up to Chardae's freshly built three bedroom, two bathroom home. A few days after the accident, I called up Pablo and asked him to build me another house. I gave him my black card, so he could buy all of the supplies they needed and the following week, Chardae was moving in. Ya'll think people be bullshitting when they tell you how hard and fast Mexicans work but they aren't. Those guys built the house and painted the walls in a couple of days!

Chardae

These past two weeks with Rashard have been nothing short of amazing! Yea, he has his moments where he acts like I'm just someone he's fucking but when it comes down to the baby, he's a whole nother dude. I love the father in him, which is why I'm not going to let him go. My biggest fear is that he will leave me to be a single mother and I'll be back in the projects fucking the dope boys to pay my bills.

I was stripping down at the Foxy Lady when I met Rashard, so I never needed him to give me anything but dick. Thank God, I was able to quit before he found out about it. After I heard him talking about how he'd never date a stripper seriously because he wouldn't want other niggas looking at his girl, I ran down to Foxy Lady and gave Skee my walking papers. He begged me to stay because I was his main attraction but I had a baller to pull.

I had everything planned down to the T about how I would trap him. I had to gain his trust, so the first couple of years, I had an unopened box of condoms in my drawer, in case he forgot to bring one when he came over. Then, eventually, I would just pour the condoms out in my drawer and he would inspect them on the low. Then, his visits became far and few in between, so I went down to the health department and got on the birth control pill. Word began to circulate about Rashard and some chick he goes to school with that ain't from here. I didn't find out until after I was already pregnant that they weren't dating yet. See, as soon as he showed interest in the chick, Twan told me what was up but I didn't know he was lying!

So, me being me, I sat the condoms under my lamp so the heat from the bulb could dry it out enough to break while we're fucking. I threw them back in my drawer and when he came over, we turnt up! We were so fucked up; I don't even remember if we used a condom or not but that's when I got pregnant. I knew the day I missed my first period that I was pregnant, but I was too afraid to tell him. Then, this nigga started messing around with her. Next thing I know, he's taking her out on dates and got her hosting parties and every damn thing, and that's what gave me the courage to tell him I was pregnant.

I don't know what happened to them these last few weeks and frankly, I don't give a damn. All I know is, one day, Rashard limped his ass in my house and told me let's go, and I happily left with him. I got the shock of my life when we pulled up here, our new home. Well, he never stays all night but he comes running whenever I call him. The thing about that is, whenever someone else calls him, he runs to them too. I don't know what's going on but I'm going to find out today because what he's not going to do is play with my feelings.

As I stood in the doorway of my new beautiful three bedroom, two bathroom home, I realized how blessed I am to have him in my life. Just because I'm pregnant, he had this house built from the ground up! It's super nice too; I've never seen a place this nice before. When you first walk in, you walk into the living room and it's huge! It's equipped with a black leather sectional that goes around the entire living room. There's a 61" plasma TV mounted on the wall with a huge frame that makes it looks like a big picture whenever the TV is paused. The kitchen is down the hall and to the left with all black appliances. The guest bathroom is on the right hand side of the hallway and is decorated in all black as well. Now, the guestroom is plain, housing only a queen sized bed, dresser, and TV. The baby's room has football decorations everywhere and is completely set for his arrival, stocked with a crib, rocking chair, diaper genie, and closet organizer. My master bedroom is across from the nursery and has the other bathroom in it. It has a king sized bed that I'm always in alone that sits on top of an all-black fluffy soft rug. Part of the wall was knocked out to hook the TV up inside of the wall.

"Man, why the fuck you standing in the doorway like this?" Rashard snapped, as he walked up to me with my ice cream in his hands. I had been craving butter pecan ice cream all day long and my superman brought it to me. I snatched it from his hands and padded barefoot across my hardwood floors, heading to the kitchen. I grabbed a spoon and went back to sit on my couch and watch Grey's Anatomy. "You need to stop coming to the door dressed like that," Rashard said calmly, as he sat on the couch next to me.

I looked down at my attire and knew instantly why he was upset. I had on a black tank top shirt with no bra and thongs. I was so use to walking around the Foxy Lady like this that I hardly ever realize when I'm dressed inappropriately. I really don't see shit wrong with it, but oh well. "Ok Shard," I said, as I scooped more ice cream into my mouth.

I closed my eyes to savor the taste on my tongue as Rashard began to rub my belly. I'm 23 weeks now and I've finally started feeling his kicks. As he began to bounce around and bump into Rashard's hand as he slid it across my barely visible belly, I fell in love. This is the man I want in my life. The caring, nurturing, loving Rashard. Not the one that come fuck me and leave when someone else calls Rashard.

"We need to talk," I said, as I rotated my body to face him. As much as I was enjoying the loving moment we were sharing, I needed to get to the bottom of things before I end up hurt. The mood noticeably shifted in the room and his body went stiff.

"What's up?" he asked, as he looked into my eyes. He had a slight frown on his face as he stared at me.

"What are we doing?" I asked softly. My nerves jumped on edge immediately, as I waited for him to answer.

"I'm trying to bond with my son and you're fucking with me," he said without breaking his stare. He hasn't even blinked yet.

"No, I'm not trying to fuck with you. I just don't want to get hurt," I explained. I could feel the tears welling up in my eyes. I silently cursed myself for being so emotional but this pregnancy has made me the meanest cry baby ever!

"I'm not going to hurt you but let me break it down, so it can forever be broken. I've never lied to you. We ain't together, so I don't owe you shit. What we are doing is raising my son. I bought you a house away from the hood; it's fully furnished and stocked with everything you will ever need. I bought you a car that can get you wherever you need to go; what more do you need?" he asked, as he looked at me. My tears fell at a rapid pace but they didn't seem to have any type of effect on him as he continued to stare at me. I wiped my face over and over but the tears just wouldn't stop coming.

"Do you have to always be an asshole?" I asked with an attitude.

"What you want me to do? Lie? You want me to sell you a dream about us being a happy family, getting married, and raising him in one household? Naw, I'm not doing that. My words may hurt right now but this pain is better than the pain the lies will make you feel later," he said then shrugged his shoulders.

"Fuck you!" I said because that's the only thing I could say. He was right.

I know I wanted to talk but I guess I was hoping for a different response. I want to know why I'm not good enough to have those things with him but I'm afraid of his answer. I scooped more ice cream in my mouth before I stood to my feet and walked away.

"You can't be stressing yourself out over shit you can't change ma. I love my son and because you are his mother, I love you, but we ain't gone be together," Rashard said, as he wrapped his arms around me from behind and rubbed my stomach. I closed the freezer door and removed his hands then walked off.

"I'm in love with you," I said with my back to him, once I made it in my room. I knew he was behind me because I could smell his Gucci cologne.

"You're in love with what could be. You will get over it," he said and walked away.

I stood in the same spot with my back towards my room door until I heard the front door close. The flood gates opened and tears were, once again, pouring out of my eyes. I dropped down to my knees and wrapped my arms around my body, as I continued to cry and rock.

Tamia

How dare Rashard have the audacity to ask me if I'm fucking Brandon! What the fuck kind of shit is that? I felt insulted. I can NOT believe he would think that I would have done that. I know a lot of females fuck whoever they want and whenever they want, without a care in the world. I'm not knocking them but that's not me. That never has been me! Hell, Rashard and I were dating for months before the accident and he hadn't even fucked me, so why would he think I had fucked someone else in the three weeks that he has been out!

I stormed out of the house for two reasons. The first reason is because I had just said something that I didn't mean. I would love for us to keep dating and make it together. The second reason is because I was really close to fucking him up. Knowing that he's been in a coma for three weeks and won't have any strength to fight me off is why I walked away. I'll never kick a man while he's down.

"Leaving so soon?" Doc asked, as I raced by him.

"Fuck him!" I said, as I continued to walk.

"He must have told her," I heard Doc say but I had no idea what he was talking about, so I continued to walk outside to Candy's truck. As I stood outside her truck, I decided to finally reply back to Brandon's text messages.

Brandon: i cnt believe u ditched me fo dat nigga

Brandon: will i c u later?

Brandon: so i guess u gne ignore me cuz he right thea

Tamia: don't

Brandon: don't what?

Tamia: im not in the mood for this bullshit right now

After I sent the last text message, I shut my phone off. I can't believe Brandon is acting like a bitch right now. Funny thing is, they are both worried about the other one when they should only be worried about me. I'm single, so technically, I can date who the fuck ever I want but I ain't on no shit like that. All I want to do is graduate with honors and receive my degree then land an awesome job. I just want to have a normal life where my best friend isn't kidnapped and someone isn't trying to kill me. I guess that's just wishful thinking.

My thoughts began to shift to Armani because I still hadn't seen or talked to her since before she got kidnapped. Now that the world is free of Steve, we can live peacefully without looking over our shoulders. "Damn, I miss her retarded ass," I said out loud to myself. Armani and I were inseparable back in the day and I still don't know what drove us apart. What did I ever do to her to make her hurt me?

"You good?" Candy asked, as she strolled out of Doc's house. She had a slight frown on her face, so I'm sure she's upset and just trying not to show it.

"This was not at all the reunion I envisioned," I responded.

She used the remote to unlock her doors so I hopped in. "Hopefully, it gets better. If not, just remember to always do what makes Tamia happy; no matter how it makes others feel," she said. I had a feeling her words had way more meaning behind them than she was letting on. I shook the feeling I had and focused on my nails, which needed a desperate fill in.

"How about we go to the nail salon?" I suggested. When I glanced over at Candy, she was inspecting her nails in the same manner I had just done.

"Let's do it," she said, as her phone started to ring. We both glanced at it at the same time and saw Twan flash across the screen. She hit a button on her steering wheel to take the call.

"This is Candy," she said in an annoyed tone.

"Where you been baby? I've been looking for you," his voice boomed through the speakers.

Candy reached over and turned the radio down as she sighed dramatically. "Around. What do you need?" she asked, as she continued to drive. I stared out the window and pretended as if I wasn't listening.

"I need you baby. I just ran into ya boy," he said then paused. "Nigga was in the grocery store buying ice cream," he said with a laugh. Candy laughed nervously but I don't know why she was nervous about Deuce buying ice cream.

"Well ok, I'll hit you up later," Candy said and hit a button on the steering wheel to disconnect the call.

When I glanced over at her, she had this spaced out look in her eyes, like she wasn't really here with me right now. Whatever she's going through is really taking a toll on her. "Candy, you know I'm your friend right and I love you," I said, as I looked at her. She nodded her head but didn't take her eyes off the road. "You have been there for me since I met you and I just want you to know, whenever you're ready to talk, I'm here," I said, just to let it be known that she can count on me the same way I can count on her. She nodded her head then turned into Angelic Nail & Bar.

I hopped out of her truck as fast as I could in true thirsty lady like fashion! Ha! This is the first nail salon I'd ever been to that serves liquor. As soon as we walked in and told them what we were getting, we were handed a glass of mimosa. We both sat down next to each other in massage chairs as we soaked our feet. Two Asian ladies came over and poured bath beads inside the water, giving it a silky feeling.

I pulled my phone out and powered it back on just as Michelle and her cousin came strolling in. I watched them like a hawk as they told the greeter what they were getting and had a seat in the waiting area. "Candy, I thought everybody get a drink when they come in," I said.

"Girl no! You have to be spending at least $30 to get a drink," she said, as I looked over at them again.

"Mmmmhhh," was my response.

My phone vibrating in my hand caught my attention. It was vibrating so long, I thought it was ringing. When I glanced down at it, my text messages were doing numbers! I waited until it stopped vibrating and sighed heavily when I saw they were all from Brandon. "What's wrong?" Candy asked with her eyes closed. I could tell she was enjoying her massage and I was so caught up in my phone that I didn't realize I was getting mines.

"Brandon's buggin. He's been buggin since I told him Rashard's awake," I said then felt someone looking at me. I looked up and looked directly at Michelle. Her and Tiffany were staring daggers at me. I smiled and winked at them, even though I was really aggravated at the moment. Shit, I was feeling like fuck Rashard at the moment but they didn't need to know that.

"Maybe it's time to give him his walking papers then, hell. Get you one of them lame guys everybody needs in their lives," Candy said.

I could still feel Michelle staring at me. "Hey Michelle. How are you doing sweetie? Do you need something?" I asked. I raised my voice so she could hear me.

"Tamia! Chill out!" Candy said, as she laughed and shook her head at me.

"Hey," Michelle said as she waved. "No, shut up hell!" Michelle said. I looked at her crazy because I didn't even see Tiffany's mouth moved.

"Did you see that?" I asked Candy.

"No, what?" Candy asked, as she looked up from her phone.

"Nothing," I said because she won't believe me any damn way.

I checked the time on the clock on the wall and it was nearing 2pm. I have to be at work at 7 tonight and I don't get off until 7 tomorrow morning. The closer I get to graduating, the more they throw me on the schedule. I could have kept last week my last day but I really want to land a job there once I graduate.

After our nails and toes were done, we headed out the door. Michelle and Tiffany had both gotten their toes polished and left long ago. "Where to?" Candy asked, as she cranked her truck.

"Home. I work tonight," I said, as I powered my phone back.

Candy and I talked about Brandon and those messages he sent me all the way home. Candy said he's crazy and that I should leave him alone, but I think he just doesn't know how to handle emotions. His messages ranged from apologizing about how he came at me earlier to cursing me out, back to apologizing, and back and forth until he finally stopped texting altogether.

We pulled up to Candy's house and I hopped straight in the shower and went to bed, so I'd be energized at work. When I woke up, it was 6pm so I got dressed, brushed my teeth, and pulled my hair into a tight ponytail. I wore my purple scrub pants with the matching Scooby Doo top. I topped it off with my all white classic Reebok shoes. You absolutely cannot go wrong with those.

When I got to work, we were so busy. I was stationed in the ER as a diversified technician and they ran me half past dead. We were so busy, the charge nurse, Amanda, had to stop me and tell me to go take a break. By that time, it was already 4:30am so when I returned from my break, I only had 2 hours left. I worked those with a breeze and headed back home to go to sleep.

Candy

*** Graduation Day ***

I woke up bright and early because I agreed to do Tamia's hair the day of her graduation. She had been working like a slave at the hospital and didn't want to spend her free time in a hair shop all day. I pulled a chair out and set everything up before I went to her room to wake her up. You would think she'd be so excited she couldn't sleep, but she just worked four twelve hour overnight shifts in a row. Yesterday was her first off day but we were at her old apartment cleaning it out. She's been staying with me so long, I thought she had given her notice to the apartment manager but she and Armani had already paid the lease up, so all of their things had just been sitting there.

It took us from 8am until 6pm to move everything out of it and sell all of the furniture, then clean it out. When we made it back home, Tamia took a shower and I hadn't heard a peep out of her since. I walked in her room as I knocked on her door and couldn't help but laugh at her. She was hanging upside down, halfway off the bed. I had no idea how she hadn't fell.

I grabbed her shoulders and tossed her on the bed. This crazy ass girl jumped up swinging. She almost got me good too but I ducked and jumped back. "Oh shit, I'm sorry Candy!" she said, once she got her bearings together. "I had been waking up throughout the night thinking somebody was in here with me," she explained.

"It's cool, but only because you didn't connect. I'm too fast," I said with a laugh. Now, had she connected, we would have been in here fighting. I don't care how crazy her little ass is.

"C'mon, so I can do your hair. Oh yea, Rashard wants you to meet his mama today," I said, as I stared at her intently. They hadn't talked since the day at Doc's house almost two weeks ago. He hadn't contacted her and she hadn't contacted him. The difference is he's been asking me about her, but she's just been focusing on herself. I was too proud of my girl for not folding and hitting Rashard up but I've been even more proud of her for cutting Brandon off.

"I'm not up for meeting his family. For what?" she asked, as I walked out of her room.

"Get up and c'mon woman!" I yelled over my shoulder. About fifteen minutes later, she came walking out of her room still wearing her pajamas. "Bitch, it took you fifteen minutes to get out of bed?" I asked because I don't see a difference.

"Naw bih! I pissed and brushed my teeth," she said as she sat down in my chair.

"So, I created a Facebook page, right," she said, which was news to me. She's never been one to dwindle in social media. Hell, she found out about Lisa being pregnant through Facebook but not through her own.

"What made you do that?" I asked but she shrugged her shoulders in response. She flipped through her photo albums and showed me all of the pictures she has posted so far and I can tell she's loving Facebook already but something seems off.

"So, what's the problem?" I asked.

"Chardae sent me a friend request," she said and turned to look at me. I had to fix my face because anger quickly set it when she said that.

"What the hell? Girl, don't worry about that hoe," I said, as I began to braid her hair for the sew in I was about to slay.

About two hours later, I was done and my bitch's hair was on fleek! Hell, she could throw her gown on over her pajamas and still be on point. I made her lay across the couch and plucked her eyebrows then beat her face. She took a selfie and posted it immediately on Facebook.

My phone started ringing and it distracted me from the Facebook junkie on my couch. I walked off to go get it and was surprised to see Brandon's name flashing across my screen. "Hello?" I answered the phone.

"You told her to stop talking to me," he said, as more of a statement than question.

"No," I said. "Tamia's grown; she does what she want," I said because he hadn't said anything.

"Hook us back up," he demanded.

"Man, I ain't getting in ya'll bullshit," I said with my face balled up in anger.

"You looking good Candy. You walk around with a crop top and booty shorts on all the time?" he asked. I could feel my heart beating harder in my chest as I looked around my room. "Tell Tamia it's not safe how wild she sleeps. She almost fell out the bed like four times last night," he continued. I could feel a lump form in my throat and the hairs on the back of my neck stand up. Panic set in once I realized he had been inside without either of us knowing it.

"Candy!" he called out in a raspy tone. I wanted to answer him but my voice was caught in my throat. "I know you're there Candy; I can hear you breathing. Hook us up or else," he said then hung the phone up. I immediately called Deuce but he didn't answer the phone for me. That was something he had been doing more and more lately, ignoring my calls.

I know I need to tell Tamia but I can't be the one to ruin her day. This is her big day, the day she has been waiting for, and I can't ruin that. I sat down on my bed, not having a clue of what to do until Tamia was ready to go.

Armani

Crash! Jumping out of my sleep, I had never been so afraid in my life. I can't believe he found me so fast. "How did he get passed the security desk?" I asked myself, as I climbed slowly out of bed. I began to look around the room frantically for something to defend myself with. There was nothing available but the damn remote control to the TV. After I grabbed it, I padded softly across the floor heading towards the sound.

"Boy, you scared the fuck outta me!" I snapped at Joe, breathing a sigh of relief.

"Shut up and come suck this dick," he said, slurring his words. Not wanting to piss him off while he was drunk and end up homeless, alone, and on the run, I walked swiftly to him before dropping down to my knees. I took all of him in my mouth and began to suck vigorously, as if my life depended on it. He was moaning and groaning but twenty minutes into sucking his dick, he still hadn't cum. Now, I know my head game fire so his drunk ass is going to have to fuck me.

"The fuck you doing?" Joe asked after I stood to my feet.

"My jaws tired," I said, turning around and making my ass clap for him. *Smack!* My clit jumped as Joe slapped both ass cheeks simultaneously, as I twerked in front of him. He slid his hands up my back before pushing me over. I used the table in front of us for balance as he entered me roughly. Joe was going crazy, smacking ass and pulling hair. It hurt so good; I didn't know what to do. I started throwing this ass back, meeting him halfway with every stroke. "Ouch Nigga! The fuck you doing?" I asked, jumping away from him. This nigga stuck his whole damn finger in my ass.

"Bitch, bring your ass back over here!" he yelled. His smooth deep voice echoed against the walls, causing me to jump. We stood staring at each other like we were ready for war.

"Don't touch my ass," I said, as I looked away. *Whap!* He slapped me so hard, I flipped over the coffee table and landed on the floor.

"Don't tell me what to do. You just do what I say," he stated calmly, then walked slowly to me. He had an evil aura about him as he walked closer to me. He got down on his knees and I kicked him as hard as I could in the chest, causing him to flip backwards. I hopped up and ran but he was too fast for me. I felt him grab my hair before pulling me back to him. He wrapped my hair around his fist and slammed my head into the wall over and over again.

I was starting to feel dizzy when his phone began to ring. He tried snatching his hand out of my hair but it was tangled. He dragged me to the kitchen kicking and screaming. He used a knife to free his hand by cutting my hair off, so he could answer the phone. I laid on the floor crying but listening to his one sided phone conversation.

"Where that nigga at?... Word?... Damn Amere... He made it? Well shit, I need somebody else to help me then. It's another guy?... Rashard? I don't know him.... Iight, I'ma get this lil bitch to follow him.... Iight bet," Joe said into the phone before hanging up. "Get up, let me talk to you," Joe said to me. I didn't respond right away because I was wondering if he was talking about my Amere.

"Ouch! Shit!" I yelled out, balling my body up because Joe kicked me in my side.

"Don't make me tell you again," he said with such finality before walking over to the couch.

I sat up slowly, wondering what I had gotten myself into yet again. My head was pounding and blood was trickling down my face. That kick to the side made it hard for me to breathe as I made my way to Joe slowly. "Aye, I got some shit going on that I need your help with," Joe said, as I nodded my head. "I'm fina take over these streets and all I need you to do is keep an eye on one of the boss' soldiers and wait for him to lead you to the boss," he explained.

"Sounds simple enough," I responded.

"His name Rashard. You gotta figure out how to find that nigga and trail him til he lead you to the one in charge," Joe said, not knowing I already know who Rashard is and how to find him.

Rashard and my sponsor, Vincent, were both messing with this chick name Chardae that lives in the projects. Well, she used to live in the projects, but word on the streets is, Rashard packed her up and moved her out. Rashard is also dating Tamia. If I find him, I'm sure I'll find her and what better way to hurt her than to take away her happy ending. *Yeah, I'll follow Rashard until he leads me to the man in charge and then I'm going to kill him*, I thought to myself. "Ok," I said, smiling to myself.

"You love me?" Joe asked, catching me off guard.

"Huh?" I asked, looking crazy. *I just met this nigga a few weeks ago why the fuck he think I love him?* I thought to myself.

"If you can huh, you can hear mufucker! Do you love me?" He snapped, looking at me like he will kill me if I don't. I slowly shook my head no, since I didn't want to lie to him. "NO?!" he yelled, jumping to his feet.

"Yea... uh... yes, I do," I said, deciding to just play along until I didn't need him anymore. *I'm going to have to kill this nigga too*, I thought to myself.

"That's good baby. I love you too. You're gonna be everything to me," he said, smiling before he walked away.

"The fuck man!" I said softly to myself while shaking my head. When he returned, he cleaned the blood off my face and gave me medicine for my head. Afterwards, he carried me to the bathroom to give me a bath before putting me to bed, literally. This nigga tucked me in and everything. The next couple of days, he nursed me back to health before sending me off on my mission.

Mission Destroy Tamia's life has now started.

****

I've been following Rashard for almost two weeks now and when I say he's a busy guy, I'm not playing! This nigga dick must be made of gold because he's slanging it to four different bitches! Shit, he got me wanting to see what all the hype is about. I can't believe he's still messing with Chardae because it's been years now. He done upgraded her hoodrat ass and got her living in a nice house near the city. She must be happy with him because she's getting fat. Now, Tiffany little extra hoe ass with all them damn kids knows she needs to stay away from dick period, but he been fucking off with her too. Well, I don't really know what he's doing with Tiffany because he's never inside her house long. I don't know that other girl's name but she's really pretty with a caramel complexion and hazel eyes. Tamia gotta be the most special to him because he bought the bitch a new car for graduation. We spoke briefly at graduation because she saw me lurking, so I had to put on that *I'm so happy you did it* front.

I sat in the stands because I knew with a graduating class of 210 students, I would be here for a while. "I'm tired of following him and not getting a taste of him," I thought to myself as I kept my eyes trained on his back as he walked across the stage. I often found myself fantasizing about the man everyone seems to need. A soft moan escaped my lips as my hands found their way to my pearl. The bullhorn behind me snapped me back into reality, which was great because I did not need to be getting myself off at a damn college graduation.

After graduation was over, I walked out onto the field to meet the graduates halfway, along with damn near everyone in the stands. I can't lose him again because last time, Joe beat me to sleep and when I woke up, he had done cleaned me up and place me in bed. Anyway, when I spotted him, I got as close as possible without seeming out of place, being as though I wasn't speaking to anyone. "Mani?" Tamia asked, catching my attention. I hadn't realized she walked up to me because I was so into watching Rashard mix and mingle with different people.

"Congratulations boo!" I said, wrapping my arms around her neck, all the while watching Rashard.

"Thanks. I can't believe you're here," she stated dryly.

'I'm not here for you,' is what I wanted to say. "Girl, I wouldn't miss your big day for nothing in the world," *I said with the brightest fakest smile I could muster up.*

"Tamia!" *Rashard began to yell, looking around for her.*

"Tamia, do you hear him calling you?" *I asked her, noticing the awkward look on her face.*

"He wants me to meet his family. I gotta get outta here," *she said*

"Wait. Here, put your number in my phone," *I said, as I shoved my phone in her hand. She hesitated then entered her number and stormed off towards the exit.*

"Were you just talking to Tamia?" *some stripper looking bitch walked up to me asking.*

"Yes. She said she didn't wanna be anywhere near ya'll and left," *I answered, throwing my twist in there. The chick didn't say anything in response, as she turned to head back to the group surrounding Rashard.*

Beep! Beep! The car behind blew the horn, letting me know the light had turned green and I hadn't drove off yet. Somehow, Rashard had lost me again and I was driving around trying to find him, instead of going home like I normally do when he shakes me. I'm just not trying to face Joe angry again. I'd rather be with Steve than him, at this point, because he treats me far worse. I'd rather be sprayed with that water hose multiple times a day than to take the beatings Joe gives me when I make him mad. He's got me walking around on eggshells, trying not to piss him off. I need to hurry up and hurt Tamia, so I can find Dave or Vincent and get the hell away from Joe's ass, and I've got the perfect person to help me.

Michelle

I haven't been to work in I don't know how long, but it's ok because Twan has been helping me in exchange for helping him out. We all support each other, no matter how twisted you may think we are. We are joined together by a common enemy and that makes our bond stronger. Twan paid my lease up and every time I bring him more information, he tosses more money at me. I have been following Tamia since the day after we all met Lisa at the hospital. I hate how happy she is about life, like she isn't the cause of so many people's pain! Karma is taking far too long to catch up to her, so I'm going to intervene.

Tiffany has been treating me like a fucking basket case since that day at the nail shop when Tamia spoke to me. I tried to play it off like I was talking to her but she had caught me talking to myself. I had been doing pretty good in front of people when the voice starts talking. I simply ignore her and continue on with whatever I was doing. That day, being so close to Tamia and not being able to get my revenge, was taking a toll on me mentally. I'm not crazy though. A lot of people talk to themselves.

"Where to?" Tiffany asked, as we pulled away from UMA's graduation. As crazy as it is, I still love Ray and I was not about to miss his big day for nothing in the world. He was surrounded by so much love from his family members. The only one that wasn't there was Bo and we all know Bo hates Ray. I saw Tamia but she was nowhere near Ray or his family, which led me to believe there's trouble in paradise. Well, that and the reason that she's kicking with Brandon.

"Let's see where Ray is taking that Benz truck he bought," I said. Tiffany pulled to the side of the rode. About thirty minutes later, I saw Candy drive out the parking lot in the Benz and we followed suit. We followed her all the way to the house she shares with Tamia.

"He bought that truck for Candy?" Tiffany asked.

"No bitch, the tag says Tamia!" I said, as I pointed at the tag on the truck.

The ringing of my phone distracted me from our conversation. "Yea?" I answered, annoyed because whoever was calling had blocked their number.

"Michelle, let's work together," a female voice said over the phone.

"And do what?" I asked, as I hit Tiffany to get her attention.

"Put it on speaker," she whispered to me. I put it on speaker phone and laid the phone down on the middle console.

"Taking Tamia out so you can get your man," the voice said. I glanced up at Tiffany, just as she was rolling her eyes.

"Let's meet right now," I said because I don't like this secret shit. I need to know who I'm talking to.

"Where?" she asked. I quickly gave her Tiffany's address and disconnected the call.

"Let's go to your house," I said. Tiffany pulled off as we headed to her place. "The kids not there, are they?" I asked, not wanting to put her children in any danger.

"Naw, my mama got em," she answered, as she drove recklessly all the way to the projects.

When we pulled up, I noticed the girl immediately as the girl that was on the news for getting kidnapped. "I'm Michelle and this is my cousin, Tiffany," I said and watched her mouth drop. "Why she looking like that?" the voice said, but I ignored it and the look and followed Tiffany inside. I gestured for Armani to follow us once she stopped staring at Tiffany. *Maybe she likes girls*, I thought to myself as I walked inside.

"Bitch, you need to start cleaning up more often! Yo shit ain't never company ready," I said, as I shook my head. She had toys and dirty clothes all over the living room floor. I was literally either stepping over something or kicking something else out of my way my entire walk to her couch. I grabbed the pizza box off the couch and handed it to her. She tossed it on the floor behind the couch and sat on a pile of clothes. I shook my head and shot the girl an apologetic look.

"I'm Armani," she said, as she used her purse to knock the clutter out of the chair she was about to sit in. She shocked me when she shook her head and remained standing.

"Ain't shit gone bite you!" Tiffany snapped at her.

"Shit, you can't guarantee that! Look what I got on. I ain't tryna have no bed bugs crawl up in my pussy; hell, I'm already not wearing panties," she snapped back, then crossed her arms across her chest.

"Nasty bitch!" Tiffany mumbled to herself and we both shot her a look.

How the fuck can Tiffany fix her mouth to call anybody nasty? Talk about ridiculous. I noticed Armani hadn't taken her eyes off of Tiffany yet. "So, what's your plan?" I asked Armani.

"Simple. I just want to hurt Tamia by taking away her happy ending. I wanna kill Rashard in front of her," she said, like it would be that easy. She obviously doesn't know Rashard. He's smarter than she's giving him credit for.

"Girl please, she got a sexy happy ending lined up name Brandon. That's who she been kicking it with for at least two weeks," I said to her.

I watched her slouch her shoulders as she began to think then she looked up, like she was confused. "What's on your mind?" I asked because I don't like how she's been looking since we got out the car.

"I'm confused," she said, as she looked between Tiffany and I. She shook her head then shifted her weight from one leg to the other.

"What's the problem?" I asked, as I looked over at Tiffany. She rolled her eyes at Armani and shook her head.

"Why are we even talking to her?" Tiffany asked. "She's standing there like she thinks she's better that us and-"

"No bitch, I'm standing here like this filthy bitch need to clean her fuckin house up! Don't come for me, baby girl, because I promise you, you won't like my return policy!" Armani snapped as she cut Tiffany off.

I looked at Tiffany and noticed her right eye was twitching and I didn't want things to escalate any more than they already had. "C'mon, ya'll stop. Armani, what's confusing you?" I asked, as I tried to direct the conversation back to where it was heading. Armani closed her eyes and took a deep breath before she responded to me.

"You're Rashard's ex, right?" she asked. I nodded my head but I could feel my heartbeat speed up. My heart was beating so hard in my chest that I could feel it in my throat.

"So, what ya'll were doing threesomes or something?" she asked with confusion written clearly on her face. I looked at Tiffany and did not like the look she had on her face.

"Ooooh no, say it ain't so!" the voice screamed in my ear. "What you mean?" I asked, without taking my eyes off of Tiffany.

"Are ya'll both sleeping with him or did you just pass the buck off to your cousin?" she asked, like it was no big deal.

I could feel the tears welling up behind my eyes. My heart was about to leap out of my mouth and my head was pounding. "Bitch, I'm not sleeping with Rashard!" Tiffany snapped. I began to calm down because I know when she's telling the truth. As I watched her shoot daggers at Armani, I could tell she was not sleeping with him. I breathed a sigh of relief as I focused my attention back on Armani.

She had this smirk on her face like she knew something we didn't. "Kill her," the voice said. "Kill who?" I asked, as I stared down at the floor. "Don't be stupid," the voice said.

"Who are you talking to?" Armani asked, as she took a step back closer to the door.

"Huh?" I asked, like I didn't know what she was talking about. When I looked over at Tiffany, she had fear written all over her face and I began to wonder why would she be afraid.

I left out of the room and when I returned, Armani was still there. "Why did you think she was sleeping with Ray?" I asked.

"Ray? Oh Rashard? Shit, he's over here enough. Probably just sucking his dick," she said with a shrug.

"N... n... no, I wasn't!" Tiffany yelled. I looked down at her right hand and noticed she was rubbing her thumb across the fingertips of her other fingers. That was always my telltale sign to know when she was lying.

"How long?" I asked, as I refocused my attention on Tiffany. She looked at Armani with pleading eyes before she looked at me. She didn't respond. I stood to my feet and walked over to her as she coward into the corner of the couch. "How long?" I asked through clenched teeth. "Just kill her!" the voice said. "Shut the fuck up; I got this!" I responded.

"Mimi, it's not what you think. She's lying," she said as she held her hands up.

I pulled the knife from behind my back and sliced both hands open. I watched blood leak from her palms and she screamed out in pain. "Oooh shit," Armani said but I can't worry myself with her right now.

"How long?" I asked again.

"Five or six years Mimi; I don't know," she said, as she tried to scoot her body away from me. She flipped over the arm of the couch and hurt her hands more than they already were.

I swung the knife again, only this time, I sliced her back. She flipped over in pain as she cried and began to scoot away from me again. I took a step closer to her every time she thought she was about to get away. "Don't do this Mimi. I'm your cousin," she pleaded. I couldn't remember the last time she called me Mimi. In fact, I stood in front of her trying to recall the last time she called me that. Eventually, I shrugged my shoulders and took another step towards her.

"Were you my cousin when you fucked Ray?" I asked, as I swung the knife and sliced her arm. She groaned out in pain as she tried to close the gash with her hand. "Were you my cousin when you were going behind my back to suck his dick?" I asked, as I swung the knife again and sliced her across the chest. "No, I don't think that fact ever crossed your mind," I stated, as I stepped down on her stomach. I raised my foot and slammed it down as hard as I could in her stomach over and over until she started throwing blood up.

I removed my foot and watched her slither towards the door like the snake she has always been. "Kill her already! You're boring me," the voice said, then I heard a stifled yawn. I walked over to Tiffany and sat down on her stomach and stabbed her in the mouth. She started gurgling the blood that was spewing from her mouth wound. I smiled brightly as she swung her hands weakly, finally deciding to fight back.

"I'm sorry," she said, as she continued to spit blood out of her mouth.

"It's too late to apologize. It's too late," I sang with a smile on my face as tears streamed down my cheeks. "You never did like my singing, did you?" I asked, as I placed the knife on her throat. She started to get buck like a bull, trying to throw me off of her. I grabbed her shirt and held on with one hand in the air as I rode Tiffany.

"Ah fuck! 10 seconds," I said after I fell off.

"Bitch is fucking looney," Armani said. I had completely forgot she was there watching.

"Kill her too," the voice said. "I am," I replied as I grabbed Tiffany, who had flipped over and tried to crawl away. I stood up with her hair clenched tightly in my fist as I pulled her head back as far as it would go. "Aaaaaaaaarrrrggghhhh!" I screamed as I slit her throat open. Blood began to gush out as I let her go and she hit the floor as dead as a door knob.

I looked up at Armani and as much as I hate to kill her at this moment, I know I can't let her leave here. I stood upright and charged at her without a second thought. I had my knife raised above my head, ready to make it a quick death for her, when I felt a powerful blow to my stomach. As soon as our eyes connected, I realized she had kicked me in my stomach. I doubled over in pain and dropped the knife.

Wham! She hit me so hard on the top of my head, I saw stars. I wobbled slightly and I could feel my body falling forward until she hit me again. I flipped over the couch and landed on a toy. "Fuck!" I said out loud because the shit hurt like hell. I rubbed my back as I rolled over onto my knees but she kneed me in the chin before I could get up and sent me flying backwards. "You need a gun for this bitch," the voice said. Armani jumped on top of me and punched me over and over. It felt like I was being jumped because her blows were landing everywhere. I started to feel woozy and I could see black spots, then everything went dark.

Tamia

My big day was amazing! It's official, ya girl has a degree in Healthcare Administration! Now I can be somebody's boss while they do all of the leg work I've been doing all of my life. I'm so proud of myself for not allowing myself to fall victim to society. I'm living proof that it doesn't matter where you come from, it's all about where you're going. I grew up in the hood, born fatherless, and became motherless before I made it to high school. I was forced to grow up way before my time! The deck of cards was stacked against me from birth but I played my hand the best way I could and came out on top.

As I looked into the crowd of people here to support the graduation class, tears formed in my eyes because nobody was here for me. I quickly swallowed that self-pity up because it wasn't going to get me anywhere and I was not about to allow anything to take away from my day, including Rashard.

Candy told me he was ready for me to meet his family but how could that be when he wasn't even ready to be mature enough about being in a relationship. I can feel that he was hiding something and I think Candy knows exactly what it is that he's hiding. That's why there was so much tension between the two back at Doc's house. Whatever it is that he's hiding, I don't blame Candy for not telling me because for one, she was his friend first and two, it must be extremely hard being in the middle of our bullshit.

I've been seeing the worry lines on Candy's face but I don't want to assume why they're there, so I need her to tell me. If they have anything to do with me, I need her to wash those lines away because the worst thing you can do is beat yourself up over things you can't change. I don't know what happened to her after she finished my hair this morning, but she's been acting paranoid ever since. When I asked her what her problem was, she didn't answer me.

"Congratulations Boo, we did it!" Allison said, as she jumped up and down and then gave me a hug.

"Thanks girl, same to you," I said, as my eyes landed on Armani.

"I'm sorry Allycat but I see a familiar face," I said to her before I made my way through the crowd. I had Allison in two classes during the fall semester and we got close but only at school when it came to school work.

I walked up to Armani slowly and was shocked that she showed up. Something wasn't sitting right with me about her presence but I shook it off. When Candy called my name, I had to dip out before she tried to introduce me to Rashard's family. I don't think anything is wrong with his family but there's really no reason for us to meet at this point, considering we still aren't in an actual relationship; hell, we haven't even been talking! I tried just running away but Armani shoved her phone in my hands. I looked down at the phone then up at Armani. I looked all over her face and saw bruises that looked like they were healing. I looked at her neck and saw a small bruise on the side and entered my number in her phone. Call me stupid but she looks like she could use a friend.

I stormed off towards the parking lot before Candy caught up to me. It wasn't until I reached the parking lot that I realized I rode with her. "Ugh! Shoot, I gotta start driving myself," I said out loud to myself, as I pulled my phone out to call a cab. I walked aimlessly through the parking lot until I ran into Rebecca, a girl that was in my physics class.

"Hey Becky, can I get a ride?" I asked, as she unlocked her doors. She looked back at me at and smiled, then gestured for me to hop in on the passenger's side. Rebecca is a slim, light skinned chick with high cheek bones, smoke grey eyes, and a model like body. She was majoring in nursing and now she just needs to go to nursing school, and she'll be finished.

"Are you happy it's finally over?" she asked, as she maneuvered through the pedestrians heading to their vehicles.

"Yes! Thank God! We did it!" I said.

"Want to go out and eat?" Rebecca asked, but I started to feel extremely weird about being around her all of a sudden.

"Naw, I'm not really feeling good," I said, as I rubbed my stomach. "Tomorrow definitely, though. Let me put my number in your phone," I said as I held my hand out.

"No!" she said, too fast for my liking. I gave her the side eye as she quickly corrected herself. "Just save my number in yours," she said, attempting to save face. I pulled my phone out and waited for her to recite her number, so I could key it in. Once I saved it, I shot Candy a 911 text and told her who I was with so if I didn't make it home, she knew where to look.

I gave Rebecca directions to my old place and she headed in that direction. She grabbed a bottle of water and dropped her phone as she did but didn't realize it. I didn't pay it much attention as she continued to drive and drink from her bottle. "Want one?" she asked and pointed to the back. I'm not sure what she could have done to an unopened bottle of water but I wasn't about to take a chance and drink any of it. "I'm ok," I said, as her blinking phone caught my attention.

It didn't ring out loud but it was laying on the floor by my foot, lighting up with Brandon flashing across the screen. I quickly sat my purse on top of it, so she wouldn't see it. We continued riding with the radio playing softly. I glanced over at her and she looked like she was in deep thought. We pulled up to my old apartment building and climbed out of her car, making sure I grabbed her phone and my purse at the same time.

"Thanks," I said and closed the door. I waved at her as she pulled off, then I pulled my phone out and called Candy. She didn't answer the phone, so I did something I didn't want to do and called Rashard.

"Yea?" he answered.

"I'm sorry, never mind," I said because I didn't like how he answered the phone, like I was bothering him.

"Tamia? I didn't look before I answered; what's up?" he said quickly. I sighed in relief.

"I'm stranded at my old place. Can you come get me?" I asked, as I began to look around.

"I'm on my way," he said, so I disconnected the call and went to sit on my steps.

Every noise I heard had my heart about to leap out of my chest. About ten minutes later, Rashard pulled up in a red candy paint charger. I walked over to his car slowly and hopped in after I checked my surroundings. "What you got going on?" he asked as he drove.

"Something weird is going on but I can't figure out what. Something just doesn't feel right," I explained. I hoped like hell he could shed some light on my situation but he couldn't or if he could, he didn't.

"Where are we going?" I asked, once I realized we had already passed the exit to go to the house I share with Candy.

"Home," he said, as he continued to drive. I didn't say anything else until we pulled up to a baby fucking mansion! My mouth hit the floor.

"Whose house?" I asked because he said we were going home.

"Listen, I know we haven't been dating long but shit, a nigga fell for you and fell hard! I'm ready to settle down and I want to settle down with you. This is our house," he said, causing a lump to form in my throat.

I got choked up and hopped out of the car and ran up to the door but it was locked. I turned around with a frown on my face until he tossed me a set of keys. I ran inside and felt like a fat kid in the chocolate factory. The flooring all the way through the house was chocolate marble tiled floors. We had six bedrooms and each one of them had a different color scheme.

When I walked into the master bedroom, I started to cry. It had a chocolate and mint green color scheme. "Ooooh, I'm going to kill Candy!" I said, once I noticed the letters that were etched on the pillowcases. The pillow on the right side had a R on it and the one on the left had a T. I told Candy that whenever I got a man and we moved in together, I was going to steal her idea. She one upped me with this one.

"Bring your mean, crybaby ass here graduate," he said from the door. I turned around and raced into his arms. As he held me, nothing else mattered but us and our happiness. The amount of time we'd known each other didn't matter and neither did the fact that for the last two weeks, we've both been too stubborn to call the other one.

After he let me go, he gave me a real tour of the house, showing me all types of secret passages and making me remember different codes. I was beyond shocked that he would go through all of this to ensure my safety, but I'd never felt more secure in my life.

I ran back to the living room to get my purse, so I could call Candy again but Brandon's name started flashing across my screen. I hit talk because it's about time I let him know Rashard and I are together, so he can't call me anymore.

"Good job B. Candy is out!" Brandon said, as soon as I put the phone to my ear. I pulled the phone away from my ear and looked at it in confusion, just as a picture of a bloody Candy appeared on the screen.

Rashard

"Aaaaahhhh Nooo, Candy!" I heard Tamia scream after I heard something shatter. I took off in the direction of her screams and was led to the living room. She was just standing there shaking and crying as I approached her. I grabbed her by the shoulders as I inspected her body for any injuries. I pulled my .45 out as I looked around the living room, but nobody was there but her. I looked down on the floor and saw a smartphone, but the screen was shattered and had gone dark. I bent over to pick it up but it wasn't Tamia's phone, unless she got a new one. I grabbed her arm and lead her to the plush cream colored couch and sat her down.

"Did you get a new phone?" I asked, as I sat on the table in front of the couch, so I could sit in front of Tamia. She shook her head no. "Whose phone is this?" I asked her because I was trying to work my way up to why she was crying.

"Rebecca. Rebecca O'Conner," she said in a shaky tone of voice.

"Where is Candy?" I asked. I watched the tears cascade down her cheeks faster as she shrugged her shoulders. "Why did you yell out for her?" I asked, trying to remain calm but she was taking too long to tell me what was up. My approach wasn't working and she still hadn't answer my question.

I grabbed her by her shoulders and stood her to her feet. "Suck that shit up, Tamia! If Candy is hurt, you know every second we right here talking is a second she's losing! Crying ain't gone help her so cut that shit out right now! What did you see and where is Candy?" I snapped and let go of her shoulders. She closed her eyes and I couldn't tell what she was doing but when she reopened them, I saw a whole nother person standing before me.

She wiped her eyes, grabbed her purse, and headed for the door. "Let's go," she turned around and said, because I was still standing in the same spot that she left me in. "Go to Candy's house," she said, once we were in the car. I pulled off and drove like a bat out of hell.

"What happened?" I asked because I needed to know what I was walking into before I got there. Candy's family so I was going regardless, but I rather be prepared.

"While you were in a coma, I was dating Brandon, Deuce's cousin. He has something to do with this but I don't know what he's doing or why he's doing it. That was Rebecca's phone. I stole it after she dropped me off because she was acting strange, and he called her. I was fina call Candy to fuss about those pillowcases but I grabbed Rebecca's phone and Brandon called. When I hit talk, he said he had killed Candy," she said, giving me a quick rundown.

I didn't respond to her. I gripped the steering wheel so tight, my knuckles had turned white. When I pulled on Candy's street, Tamia shocked me again when she asked me for a gun. I hit a few buttons on my radio and a secret compartment came out, and she grabbed the gun out of there. I watched her take the safety off and cock the gun, allowing a bullet to drop into the chamber.

When we pulled up to Candy's house, the front door was wide open. Tamia hopped out the car before I had a chance to put it in park. I hopped out behind her and ran into the house. I searched the living room, kitchen, bathroom, and Tamia's old room and didn't see anyone. What caught my attention was a flashing tiny red light that was blinking inside of Tamia's room light. I climbed on her bed and removed the globe and found a small camera that was pointing directly over her bed.

My blood began to boil as I thought of all the things Brandon's perverted ass had seen. I snatched the camera out and threw it on the floor. I jumped down and stomped on it over and over until my phone started to ring.

"Make it quick," I said into the phone because I didn't have time for small talk.

"You shouldn't have done that," a male voice said on the other end of the phone.

"Done what? Who is this?" I asked into the receiver.

"C'mon Shard man, you're smarter than that," he replied.

"Brandon. Nigga, I'm-"

"Ah, ah, ah. No threats Mr. Peterson," he said, as he cut me off me. "All I want is Tamia. Please don't make me kill Myra before you understand I mean business. I already killed Candy," he said and hung the phone up.

I looked at my phone and dialed Myra's number. It rang over and over and with each ring, my heart thumped harder in my chest. "What, you didn't believe me?" Brandon asked, as he answered my baby sister's phone.

"If you lay-"

"Now, what did I tell you about threats?" he asked and then I heard Myra began to scream in the background.

"Ok man, ok, I'm sorry. Let me talk to her," I pleaded but it was of no use because he already hung the phone up.

I slid my phone in my pocket and punched a hole in the wall. "Rashard, come help me!" Tamia screamed. I took off towards Candy's room and saw her laying in Tamia's arms. Tamia had blood all over her. "Carry her to your car," Tamia instructed. I felt like I was having an outer body experience, as I carried a girl I grew up with to my car with thoughts of my sister weighing heavy on my mind.

Once I got her in the car, I headed to the hospital. "I gave her CPR and brought her back but her pulse is still weak," Tamia explained to me. "What else is wrong?" she asked, as she looked at me.

"Brandon has Myra," I said, without taking my eyes off the road.

"What does he want?" she asked with a look of uneasiness written on her face.

"You," I said, as I glanced over at her. She didn't respond. She just turned her body completely to the front.

We pulled up to the ER parking lot and Tamia hopped out the same way she did when we pulled up at Candy's house. She returned shortly with a doctor and a wheelchair. I watched helplessly as they pulled her from the backseat and Tamia told them what she had done when she found her. I parked my car and ran into the ER waiting area looking for Tamia but didn't see her. Being as though she works here, she's probably in the back helping them. I took a seat as I waited for some type of news.

Lisa

I've been so messed up behind losing my daughter that all I want to do is end it all and join her. I didn't even have anyone to help me with the funeral arrangements, so I didn't have one. The night I found out she died and it was my fault that she couldn't be saved, I linked up with a group of people that shared the same enemy. Tamia and Rashard must go, it's just that simple. About a week after my daughter was cremated, I had finally started feeling like my old self again.

I called Andre and he came over to my house and helped me move all of my things into his because I did not want to be there whenever Amere was released from the hospital. I moved in with him but now I see the grass isn't greener on the other side. Every time I turn around, Twan is there and he has a key, so I can't walk around like I'd like too because he's always there. It's bad enough that he's always looking at me. Then on top of that, physical abuse has come out of nowhere.

Twan called a meeting today and it's going to be here at Andre's house and from what Andre told me, he's pissed off. Apparently, he gave everybody a job to do and so far, nobody has gotten anything done. "Babe, you gone cook for the meeting?" Andre asked.

"Now you know I don't cook," I said as I gave him the side eye. I could see him clench his fist as he stared at me. "I'll order pizza," I said, as I walked away and grabbed the phone.

Whap! Andre slapped the cordless phone out of my hand and it slid across the floor with the battery hanging out of it. My hand throbbed as my bottom lip began to tremble. He hasn't always been abusive; it didn't start until he got the news that Steve was dead. Steve was his only connection to his dad and the only person who kept his dad on the right track. With Steve gone, there's no telling where his dad is or what he's doing. I tried to tell him everything would work itself out and I realize now that I shouldn't have said a word. Maybe if I had just allowed him to have his moment, the beatings wouldn't have started.

"I don't want no damn pizza! If yeen gone cook, go get some damn Popeye's or some shit!" he snapped, as he stood directly over me. He was breathing like a dragon and I could feel his hot breath on my forehead as he peered down at me.

"I... I... I don't... I don't-"

"DON'T WHAT LISA, DAMN!" he screamed and I jumped so hard that I bumped into him slightly.

"I don't have no money," I rushed out barely above a whisper.

"What?" he asked with his eyebrows crinkled as he frowned.

"I don't have no money," I said a little louder.

"You ain't worth shit," he said, as he stuck his hand in his pocket and handed me a wad of cash.

I grabbed it, slipped my shoes on, and headed to the car he got for me. It's an old beat up Volkswagen that doesn't has a key. It has a screwdriver stuck in it that I have to jam in and turn while pumping the gas to get it to crank. "I should have stayed my ass on the coast," I said out loud to myself as I got in my car. To close the driver's side door, you have to lift it up and pull hard or it will fly open while you're driving. I cranked the car up and pulled off as I wished like hell I had a seatbelt but there weren't any anywhere in the car.

When I pulled up to Popeye's, I began to dread the line that I knew would have me sitting there forever. Surprisingly, I ordered and got our food in a timely manner. I was about to pull off when someone caught my attention.

Everything about her looked so familiar as I pulled up slightly to allow the car behind me to move to the window. As she got closer, the smile on my face got wider. "Why the fuck is Tamia walking?" I asked myself out loud. She looked paranoid out of this world as she continued to walk while looking back. I looked past her to see if anyone was coming, but I didn't see anyone. I watched her like a hawk until she was directly in front of my car. Without a second thought, I pushed the pedal to the metal and my tires screeched as I took off towards Tamia.

*** Back at the house ***

I pulled up to the house a complete nervous wreck. I have no idea how to explain the damage I just caused to my car. I pulled the door latch and used my shoulder to ram the door open. I walked cautiously up the steps with the food in my hand. I took a deep breath once I was outside of the door before I walked in.

Twan, Andre, Bo, and Daphney were all present. She didn't look as dusty as she did the first time I met her outside of the hospital, so I figured Twan had been helping her out like he was helping the Michelle chick. "Are ya'll ready to eat?" I asked, as I walked in with my arms filled with Popeye's.

"Fix everybody plate and bring it to em," Andre demanded. I nodded my head and walked into the kitchen.

"Damn boy, you got her trained good!" I heard Daphney say and everybody laughed. I quickly fixed everybody plates and spit in all of their red beans and rice. I grabbed Andre's chicken and dropped it on the floor and put it back on his plate then carried it to him.

"Thanks babe," he said with a wink.

"Anything for you," I said with a smirk.

I returned to the kitchen to get Daphney's plate and took her wing and licked it then put it back and gave it to her. "Fix me some juice," she said rudely, as she snatched the plate from me. I looked over at Andre, who had a frown on his face. I could tell his anger was directed towards me because he was staring a hole in me.

"Do you want ice?" I forced out.

"Well, ion want no damn hot juice," she replied.

"Anyone else want something to drink?" I asked. Andre and Twan nodded their heads but Bo said no.

I walked in the kitchen to get Bo's and Tre's plates then returned to fix their juice. I poured Andre's juice then dropped his ice on the floor, put it in the glass, and took it to him. I went back to fix

Daphney's juice, grabbed her ice, and slipped the ice cube as deep as I could in my pussy. Then I used my pussy muscles to push it back out before it melted and dropped in her glass. I repeated it then poured Twan a glass and took it them.

"You ain't gone eat?" Andre asked, after I took my seat.

"Oh shoot, forgot about me," I said, as I went to the kitchen and grabbed two wings and a biscuit and returned to the living room. Everyone ate in silence then I cleaned up. I could hear someone knocking on the door as I finished wiping the counters off.

I walked in the living room and everyone was sitting around like they didn't hear someone knocking. "Who is it?" I asked with my ear to the door.

"Michelle," she answered. I snatched the door open and allowed her to enter. I looked at her in shock as she walked through the door with bloody clothes on. She had dried blood all over her arms, legs, and face.

"Are you hurt?" I asked her, as I closed the door. She shook her head no.

"What do we need to talk about?" she asked, addressing the group. Everybody looked at her like she was crazy as she stood there bloody like the shit was normal. "The fuck ya'll looking at like that?" she snapped in a different tone of voice, then apologized shortly after. She was using two different voices when she did it and I think everyone noticed it.

"Lisa, take her to get cleaned up and give her something to change into," Andre said.

"Fuck," I said softly to myself. He would send me to help this deranged ass girl. "C'mon Michelle. Let's get you cleaned up sweetie," I said, like I was talking to a child. She smiled softly and followed me in the bathroom. I turned the shower on after she walked in and closed the door.

"You can hop in and I'm going to get you a change of clothes ok." I said, but she didn't respond. "Michelle, are you ok?" I asked her. I touched her arm to get her to open her eyes.

"Don't fucking touch me bitch!" she said and pushed me into the mirror. It shattered all over the floor as I slowly tried to stand. "I'm so sorry," Michelle said.

"I'm ok now," she said and helped me to my feet.

I know you're wondering why I didn't hit her back but I've never been the fighting type. I've never had a fight a day in my life, so I'm not sure if I would know what to do. After she helped me up, she got in the shower fully dressed and my mouth hit the floor. "You can go get my clothes now," she said without looking at me.

I slipped out of the door and peeked around the corner into the living room. I waved my hand frantically until Andre looked at me and excused himself. "What the fuck you want?" he asked, as he stood over me. I looked up at him, trying to figure out where this guy came from and when the guy that I was falling for would come back.

"Michelle is fucking looney!" I whispered. His facial expression softened and his shoulders relaxed.

"What she do?" he asked.

I took a step away from him because I knew what I was about to say wouldn't sound like the truth. "She keeps turning into someone else and then back to herself. I don't know, she's crazy," I said, as I looked away from the angry glare he was giving me.

"Bitch, if you don't get yo gah damn ass back there and get that bitch some clothes, clean her up, and bring her back in here, so we can get this meetin ova wit ima sucka punch yo ole stupid ass!" he snapped at me with spit flying from his mouth. I turned around quickly and got her some clothes.

Tamia

After I made sure Candy was straight and in good hands, I snuck out the side entrance. I still had the gun Rashard had given me but I was not about to allow his sister to get hurt because of me. I wouldn't have blamed him had he dropped Candy off and then took me to Brandon to get his sister out safely, but he didn't do that.

As soon as I was out the side door, I sprinted to the street and didn't stop until I was a block away from the hospital. My phone started to ring and when I looked at it, I didn't recognize the number. "Where you at?" I asked, as I answered the phone because I thought it was Brandon.

"Just left the projects. Where are you because we need to talk?" a familiar voice said. I pulled my phone away from my ear and looked at the number again, but still didn't recognize it.

"Armani?" I asked, after I put the phone back to my ear.

I continued to walk and look back occasionally to make sure Rashard hadn't realized I was gone and came looking for me. "Yea. Where are you? We gotta talk," she said.

"Meet me at Popeye's down the street from the hospital."

"Ok, I'm about five minutes away," she said and disconnected the call. *I wonder what she need to talk about*, I thought to myself as I continued to walk. I kept looking back to make sure Rashard didn't come out the door and to look for Armani.

A few minutes later, I'd made it to Popeye's but I saw a bench right next to it. I decided to walk to the bench and wait, instead of going inside of Popeye's. I didn't know what she wanted to talk about but if it was private, then we wouldn't have privacy inside of one the busiest fast food restaurants I'd ever eaten in.

As I was crossing, it felt like someone was watching me. I began to look around but didn't see anybody until I was passing the exit sign. I looked to my right and saw Lisa in an old beat car. I'm not good with cars, so I can't tell you what she was driving. I focused my attention on the ground in front of me because I didn't have time for an altercation over a man I didn't want. *I did want to give her my condolences for her daughter though*, I thought to myself as I heard tires screech.

I didn't even look up. I just dove out of the way and rolled into a tumble. When I made it safely in the grass, I clenched my chest because it was beating so hard. "Bitch tried to run me over," I said, as I stood up to catch my breath. I looked at the car she was driving and laughed to myself as I went to sit on the bench. I would beat her ass but judging by the car she's driving, life is already doing just that.

I watched her back away from the pole she hit while trying to hit me and smiled at her. The front of her car was dragging as she pulled off with an unreadable expression. "That's what that bitch get," someone said. When I looked up, it was one of Popeyes' employees. "Are you ok girl?" she asked, as she walked closer to me. I nodded my head in response. "Girl, do you know her because she was trying to get you!" the girl exclaimed. She couldn't have been older than 16 years of age, which wasn't much younger than me, but I still felt old talking to her. I shook my head as I checked my elbow for bruises because it was burning. When I looked at it, the skin was gone and it was bleeding. "Well, my manager called the police," the girl said and my heart started to race. I got up and walked off down the street because talking to the cops would only slow me up from getting to Myra.

"You leaving?" the girl asked, but I kept walking. I felt my phone vibrate in my hand and noticed it was Armani's number, so I answered the phone.

"Is that you walking?" she asked.

"Yes," I said, as I stopped and turned around. When she pulled up, I hopped in and she pulled off.

"Life doing ya bad, got ya walking huh?" she asked. When I looked at her, I saw the serious expression on her face.

"Naw, I got some things I need to handle. What's up though?" I said because I'm not about to just let her in and go back to besties or no shit like that. I looked over at her again because she hadn't responded yet, and Armani is never at a loss for words. She gripped the steering wheel tighter and that's when I noticed the dry blood and sores on her knuckles.

"What happened to you?" we both asked in unison then laughed.

"You first," I said, as I turned my body so I could look at her.

"I got in a fight. Fucked around and linked up with a crazy bitch. She fucked around and killed her cousin over a nigga that don't want neither of them, then tried to kill me! I beat the fuck out that hoe and left," she said and my mouth hit the floor.

"I guess I'm not the only person with crazy shit going on," I said as I turned back to face the road.

"Your turn," she said, as she continued to drive.

"I started dating this guy, Brandon, and now he done kidnapped Rashard's sister and will only let her go if he can have me. So, that's where I was headed," I said to sum it up for her.

"Bitch, is you stupid? Fuck that nigga sister! What if he kill you?" she asked, as she looked directly at me. I glanced between her and the road to make sure we weren't going to hit anybody because she obviously didn't care about either of our lives.

"No, but she has nothing to do with it and I don't want that blood on my hands. Can you take me?" I asked her after she finally put her eyes back on the road.

"Take you where?" she asked me, like I didn't just break everything down to her.

"To Brandon!" I said with a slight attitude.

"Bitch, you buggin! Where he at?" she asked. I pulled my phone out to find out.

"I've been waiting on your call," Brandon said, as he answered the phone.

"What are you doing?" I asked.

"Nothing. I wanna see you," he replied.

"Are you home?" I asked.

"Yea," he answered.

"I'm on my way," I said and hung the phone up. I gave Armani directions to his house and she headed in that direction.

She didn't say anything to me until we pulled up to his house and she didn't pull in the driveway. "Take care of yourself Mia," she said, as she opened her arms for a hug. I hesitated but leaned over and gave her a hug.

"Ok," I said, as I stepped out of her car and watched her pull off.

I shook my head as I said a silent prayer, asking God to continue to cover me because I didn't know if this was a good decision or not. Brandon swung the door open with a huge smile on his face before I made it halfway up the driveway. He ran towards me full speed and scared me half past dead as I watched him run up to me. I didn't know if I should run away from him, towards him, or just stand still. I stopped walking and watched him run up to me. When he reached me, he scooped me up and spun me around in circles before running back towards the house with me in his arms.

As soon as we crossed the threshold, I began looking for a weapon I could use to knock him out. The problem was, I didn't know how I would get away from here other than walking, considering that, once again, I didn't drive. *I've been making some of the dumbest decisions ever!* I thought to myself as he sat me down on the couch. I had never been inside of his house before now. Normally, he would stop by and just run in and get something, and then we would leave.

"Do you want something to eat or drink?" he asked, then the smile vanished. Fear set in as he rushed to my side and grabbed my hand. It didn't take long for me to realize he was inspecting my body because of the blood on me.

"It belongs to Candy," I said, as I forced my eyes to well up with tears.

"Why are you crying if you ain't hurt?" he asked in a compassionate tone of voice.

"Because I lost my sister. I'll never forgive myself because I wasn't there to help her," I said and let the tears fall. I didn't have to fake it anymore because I really did feel like Candy's in the predicament that she's in because of me.

"It's not your fault. You don't know who she pissed off," he said to me. "Maybe she deserved to die," he said in a cold tone. My hand flew to my mouth as he sat on his knees in front of me, telling me that someone who has done nothing but be there for me deserved to die!

I'm glad she's not dead, I thought to myself. "Why you do it?" I asked with my head tilted slightly to the side.

"She tried to break us up. I told her to get us back together and she didn't even try," he explained with desperation laced through his voice.

"She did!" I said, even though she told me to stay away from him. *Wham!* He backhanded me so hard, I was dazed.

"How dare you lie to me?" he asked with a sad expression on his face.

As soon as I was no longer dizzy, I began to mentally weigh my options. I could hear him talking but I had zoned out and didn't know what he was saying. I could either sit here and let him do whatever he's going to do to me and make it easy for him, or I can fight back and make it hard for him. "Are you fuckin-" *WHAM!* I punched him with all of the strength I could muster up from my current position. He lost his balance and fell over on his butt. I leaped off the couch and landed on top of him. I started raining blows on him wherever there was an opening to connect.

Before I realized what was happening, I was in the air. I tried to grab a hold of everything I thought I could reach to stop myself but I missed everything. When I hit the wall, it knocked all of the wind out of me. As I laid there coughing, I watched Brandon stand to his feet and walk up to me. He had a blank expression on his face as he looked at me.

"Ugh!" I groaned out in pain after he kicked me in my stomach. My hands immediately went down to grab my stomach.

"Why would you do that?" he asked before he kicked me again, but this time in my leg.

"Where's Myra?" I forced out through the pain.

"That's why you here?" he asked me with an evil look on his face. I tried to sit up but the pain was too much for me to bear, as I collapsed back on the ground.

"I'm sorry Tamia. Are you ok?" he asked, as he pushed my hair out of my face. He scooped me up in his arms as I continued to groan and moan in pain. He laid me softly on the couch and then left out of the living room. My mind was telling me to leave but my body wouldn't listen.

I heard movement coming from another room then a loud slap. "Chill out lil bitch before I kill you!" I heard Brandon say. A few seconds later, he stood in front of me with a tight grip on Myra.

"Let her go," I pleaded. "You want me, let her go," I said as I looked up at Brandon. He let her arm go.

"Leave," he said to her without taking his eyes off of me.

She looked at me as if she didn't know what to do. "Go," I said, as I pointed a trembling finger at the door. She hung her head low as I watched her open the front door. I didn't look away until she was all the way out the door. I breathed a painful sigh of relief and closed my eyes.

"You just wanted me all to yourself, huh?" Brandon asked.

"Just kill me," I said in response.

"What?!" he asked.

Before I could respond, I heard glass breaking. When I opened my eyes, I saw Myra had come back and used a lamp to hit Brandon on his head. The only problem was that only seemed to piss him off. "Noooo!" I screamed because he turned around and grabbed her by her neck. He slung her small frame into the wall that he had just tossed me into. I watched her collide with the wall and hit the floor, unconscious. Her body wasn't on the floor ten seconds before he was on her. He stomped and kicked her over and over as I pulled my body off the couch.

He was so into what he was doing that he didn't know I was up until I was on his back. I dug my fingers into his eyeballs as he swung and swung, trying to get me off his back.

Armani

I felt like shit as I pulled off and left Tamia to fight a battle I had nothing to do with alone. Hell, I don't even know why I felt bad about leaving a bitch I don't even like. All I could think about was how she didn't have to help me get at Steve but she did! Hell, I just found out that Steve is dead and I'd bet my last dollar that his death had everything to do with Tamia. I had to weigh my options and figure out if having Tamia back in my life was more beneficial or not. I could go back home to Joe and get this ass whooping that he undoubtedly would give me because I lost Rashard again, or I can go back and help Tamia with hopes of getting back in her good graces.

If we get back cool, I'm sure she will let me move in with her and together, we can come up with a plan to get rid of Joe. Then, I'm going to sit her down and tell her about Michelle, so we can get rid of her too. After that, I'll get my revenge on her for all of the pain she's caused me and get rid of Rashard. I'm going to see what that dick do before I get rid of him though because I got to figure out why all of these bitches seem to be addicted to this nigga.

Once I came to the conclusion that I'll be better off in Tamia's good graces than going home to Joe, I hit a U-turn in the middle of the street. It took me a minute to find the house again because I wasn't really paying attention. When I found it, I parked in front of the house next door to it and hopped out.

I walked cautiously to the front door that was left wide open and the sight before me was pretty comical. Who I assumed was Rashard's little sister was laid out on the floor knocked out cold, while the guy, who I assumed is Brandon, was trying to sling Tamia's little ass off his back.

I crept up behind them. "Let go," I said and she did, but I think more so in shock than because I told her to. She flew into the table next to the couch. Brandon bent over in pain with his hands rubbing the shit out of his eyes. I used my elbow and jumped on his back while elbowing him in the back of his head. He went down fast but that was way too easy.

I stood to my feet and stomped him everywhere as he groaned out in pain. "I knew this nigga wasn't out!" I said out loud, as I continued to stomp him. His smart, crazy ass was pretending to be knocked out, probably so he could kill me. It wasn't long before Tamia came over and pushed me away from him.

"What the fuck you doing?" I asked her until she pulled a gun out of her purse. I watched her take the safety off and shoot him twice in his back. He laid there with blood leaking from him but he wasn't moving at all anymore. I kicked him again to see if he was dead or playing possum, and he didn't move.

"Let's go," I said, as I grabbed Tamia's hand but she snatched away from me. "The fuck!" I screamed out, getting fed up with her super save a hoe tactics.

"I'm not leaving her," she said sternly. I walked over to the girl and helped Tamia lift her up. It was dead fucking weight and I was not about to carry her all the way to my car.

"Hold on," I said, as I let the girl go and they both fell. I laughed loudly as I ran out to my car and backed up in Brandon's driveway. I ran back inside and helped Tamia up first and then she helped me grab Rashard's sister.

"She alive?" I asked Tamia.

"Barely, we gotta get her to the hospital," she said, damn near out of breath. We got her in the backseat and then drove straight to the hospital.

Michelle

I stood under the hot water in the shower, washing the blood of my favorite cousin off of my body. It's only been a few hours, give or take, since I killed her and I can already tell I'm losing control. I've always heard voices since I was younger but they stopped after my dad decided to leave. They didn't start back up until Ray started dating Tamia, so I figured if I got rid of her, they would stop again. Now, my problem is, it's not just voices anymore. Now, it's like I'm not always me; sometimes I think I'm the voice in my head. "What do I do now?" I asked myself out loud as I continued to stand under the showerhead. "You finish what they started or I will!" the voice snapped in my head.

I've noticed that since I left Tiffany's house, I do things that I actually didn't do. It's like I can see it being done but it's completely out of my control. Like when I pushed Lisa into the mirror, that wasn't me but I saw it happen. I asked myself why'd I do it when she was only trying to help, I had no answer and that's why I apologized to her.

The sound of the door opening caught my attention. When I looked in that direction, I saw Lisa had returned with clothes and a pair of scissors. "She's going to kill you. Kill her!" the voice said. I scanned the bathroom for a weapon and there wasn't one in sight. The last time I was forced to fight someone without a knife, I ended up getting beat the fuck up, so I was not about to try that again.

"Are you going to kill me?" I asked her, as she stood by the door with the scissors clenched tightly in her fist as she stared at me.

"What?" she asked with a confused look on her face. "Oh! No girl," she said after she followed my gaze to the scissors. "I'm going to cut your clothes off and clean you," she explained. I nodded my head and turned back around to stand directly under the water.

I could feel her cutting my wet clothes off my body as they clung tightly to my skin. I stood there thinking of the fun times I had with Tiffany but the memories kept fading. "Ugh!" I said because I was frustrated. Lisa jumped away from me, visibly frightened by my sudden change in demeanor. I understand she doesn't understand my thought process and maybe I'm thinking, that maybe, I just need a friend to replace Tiffany.

"I'm not gonna hurt you," I said to her, as I turned my body to face her. I could feel the remainder of my clothes slide off my body then Lisa gasped. I watched her hand fly up to her mouth as she stared at my body. When I looked down, I saw the bruises for the first time. *Damn, Armani did a number on me*, I thought to myself as I touched each bruise softly.

"Is someone beating you too?" she asked with her hand still covering her mouth.

"Too?" I asked with my eyebrow raised. She slowly raised her shirt and I could see large bruises all over her stomach. Some were old but most of them were new. I frowned at her as I tried to figure out why she would stick around when this is happening.

"Who's beating you?" I asked because I'm going to make them pay for messing with my friend. She looked down and stepped away from me like I was the one beating on her. "I want to help you," I said, as I stepped out of the tub. The water had gone cold and I was not about to stand there freezing. I walked closer to her and forced her to look up by grabbing her head and standing directly in her line of vision.

"Who's beating you?" I repeated. I watched the tears well up in her eyes. "Oh, here we go. Cry me a river!" the voice said in my head. I ignored it as I waited for Lisa to answer me.

"Andre," she said and the tears fell.

"Why are you here then?" I asked because there is no way in hell I'd stay.

"Nowhere to go," she answered sheepishly.

"You're coming with me. Let's go," I said, as I reached over her to open the door. Her jaw hit the floor as I stepped out into the hallway. "Let's go," I said and walked away. I walked into the living room and everybody was looking at me like I was crazy.

"The fuck ya'll-" Lisa cut me off by snatching me by the arm and pulling me back into the restroom.

"Girl, put some clothes on first," she said, as she shoved the clothes she brought for me in my arms.

I started laughing so hard that I had done started crying. I looked at Lisa and she was shaking her head as she laughed at me. "Check this out. Let's stay for the meeting and then I'll drive you home like you're too sick to drive yourself," Lisa said to me and I nodded my head in agreement.

Rashard

I sat in the ER waiting area aggravated beyond reproach. I had tried to call Twan and Dre, so we could find this nigga Brandon and handle them but neither one of them were answering their phones. I called Deuce and he picked up right away. I was trying not to call him because Brandon is his cousin.

"Man, you gotta get up here to Detroit Medical my nigga. Candy in the ER," I said into the receiver after he answered the phone.

"What the fuck? Shit man, she called me! What happened?" Deuce asked and the question pissed me off. I just told this nigga his girl in the hospital and he asking me what happened!

"Man, I just said Candy in the ER! If I'm calling you instead of her, then some serious shit happened, my nigga! Don't ask me no questions; say you on yo way!" I snapped on him.

"Hold on my nigga; I understand that's yo sister but I'm outta pocket right now. I'll be there when I can," he said in an aggressive but nonchalant tone. Then I heard something that let me know exactly why he couldn't come right now.

"Nigga, you wit a bitch right now?" I asked, as I jumped out of my seat. The young girl at the window shot me a look like she was scared or some shit, then picked up her phone.

I walked over to the window and snatched the phone from her and hung it up. "Bitch, don't play with me!" I snapped. "Go back there and tell Tamia to c'mere right now! She wit Candice!" I snapped on her too. I thought I heard Deuce say some unbelievable shit but I can't be sure because I was watching the girl run off to the back.

"Wait, what you just say?" I asked. I placed my finger in my ear, so I could hear him clearly.

"I said I'm with my wife! Don't disrespect her again," he said and I hung up the phone. I can't believe this nigga been playing Candy! I know she works in the club but she a good girl forreal, so she ain't deserved what he was doing to her.

"Damn man, I ain't gettin in that," I said out loud to myself.

When I turned around, the young girl came back and she had security with her. "Tamia isn't back there," she said with an attitude she didn't have before she left.

"Bitch, you think he can protect you?" I asked her and laughed maniacally. I got one sister fighting for her and another one that's been abducted; I will kill both of these bitches just for trying me right now. "Where she at?" I asked, as I took a step closer to the window.

"She left," the girl said in a fearful tone. I watched the security guard reach for his strap, so I reached back for mine. As soon as I gripped the handle, I felt a soft hand touch my hand.

"Don't. Myra needs you," she said in my ear. I removed my hand and felt her cover the handle with my shirt.

"I need another gurney," Tamia said to the girl. She took off to find help. "C'mon," Tamia said to me and pulled me outside. The person I saw was Armani and as soon as our eyes connected, she looked away. That bitch has been following me for a few weeks now and I'd been fucking with her. I'd let her follow me until I get bored and then I'd ditch her. I should have led her somewhere and just killed her, so she couldn't hurt Tamia but I didn't think about it.

"Rashard, help me," Tamia said. I snatched my eyes away from Armani and focused on Tamia in the backseat. I peered inside of the window and almost passed out from the sight of my sister laid out on Tamia's lap.

"Watch out!" a guy in scrubs yelled as they brushed passed me with the gurney. They pulled her out of the back seat carefully and rushed her to the back. I tried to follow behind them but they stopped me at the doors that lead to the back. Tamia still hadn't come in, so I walked outside and saw that Armani was helping her in from the parking lot.

My blood began to boil over as I watched her barely making it inside. *The fuck happened to her?* I thought to myself, as I did a light jog to get her. "What happened?" I asked, as I scooped her up in my arms.

"Well-"

"I wasn't talking to you!" I snapped at Armani. I heard her suck her teeth as I picked up my pace.

"Don't be like that baby," Tamia pleaded, as she looked up in my eyes.

"Why were you with her?" I asked, not caring that she could hear me.

"She needed to talk and I needed a ride," she said, as she laid her head on my chest.

"Ion fuckin like her," I told Tamia.

"Rashard!" she said and punched me in the chest.

"Alright girl, I almost dropped yo lil accident prone ass," I said and laughed.

"Says the guy that just woke up from a coma," she said playfully.

I stopped laughing and ignored that statement all together as I sat her down in the wheelchair. Her words made me think about everything that I was hiding from her and everything I was doing when I was supposed to be in a coma. I was fucking off with Chardae every now and then, but I been fucking off with Natasia heavily! Hell, I was still getting head from Tiffany. Shit, I had to do something because Tamia still hadn't even given a nigga any.

"Coma? When was he in a coma?" I heard Armani ask Tamia.

"Bitch, mind your business! Tamia don't tell her shit about me!" I snapped because all this fuckery I been committing will come out if they start talking too much.

I just realized I let the bitch follow me to all of them hoes houses before I ditched her, not ever thinking that maybe one day she will see Tamia and be messy! "Rashard, chill out," Tamia said, but she didn't answer Armani's question.

"Oh my gosh, Tamia, you wanna check in?" the girl asked and ran from behind the counter.

"Yea, she do," I answered for her. She shot a look at me but I could look at her and see she was in pain and needed to see someone. The girl stood there like she was waiting on an ok from Tamia or something. "Gone go sign her in," I said to her and she turned around and went back behind the counter.

I heard Tamia suck her teeth as I went and sat next to her wheelchair. A few minutes later, they came out to get her but wouldn't let me go back with her. They said it was because I was already waiting on someone and they didn't want me in the back roaming the halls. Straight bullshit.

Tamia

Thoughts of rather or not I'd be a fool for letting Armani back in filled my head as I was being wheeled to the triage room. I went through the triage questions without being all the way there. I don't even remember answering any of them. I was rolled back to my room and helped in the hospital bed.

"Hey Tamia. How are you feeling?" a familiar voice asked.

"I can't complain. Well, I could but it would do no good," I replied, once I looked up and saw nurse Jennifer. She chuckled softly before she responded. Her face took on a serious expression as she closed the door and walked further into my room.

"Tamia, I came down here to talk to you about work," she paused, as she looked at me with a sympathetic expression on her face. My heart sank down into the pit of my stomach as I waited for her to continue. "I'm not sure if you know this but I'm the head of the review committee. I'm also head of the hiring screening board," she said and my eyes lit up. The fact that she's at the top and I know I made a good impression on her gives me a shred of hope that all of my hard work will not be in vain.

I want nothing more than to start work now that I'm finished with school. Work and school has been my only bright spot. Since I've completed my schooling, I need to lean towards working. "Listen Tamia, the other members on the board don't want to hire you," Nurse Jennifer said and I felt like I had been gut punched.

She looked directly in my eyes as I struggled to catch my breath. The tears clouded my vision as they quickly fell from my eyes. I could feel that all too familiar lump forming in the back on my throat. "Why?" I asked halfway, knowing the answer before the question rolled off my tongue. I can only imagine how dim my once bright eyes were as I fought hard, trying to stop the tears from falling.

"Baggage. Since you started shadowing here, it has been one questioning incident after another," she said and I knew exactly what she was talking about. All of the drama in my personal life was causing me to lose the only bright spot I had left.

"Is there something I can do?" I asked because right now, I need this distraction almost as much as I need oxygen to breathe. I didn't even realize I was still crying until she gave me a box of Kleenex.

"I need you to separate yourself from the people that are bringing this negative energy into your life. Don't worry about being lonely because when you learn to separate yourself from the wrong people, you will be making room for the right ones," she said. I nodded my head as I continued to rid my face of my tears.

"I'm going to hire you based on your knowledge and work ethics. You will be on probation for 90 days. Any drama, Tamia, and you're out," she said with finality. Her tone and the look she gave me when she said it let me know that she means it.

"Thank you so much! Can you do me one more favor?" I asked with a slight smile on my face.

"Sure, what's up?" she asked. I watched her slide to the edge of her chair like she was about to receive the best gossip of her life.

"So, there's this guy I've been dating and well, umm… he's here," I said and paused to let it sink in.

"Girl, I'm not bout to lose my damn job giving you private information!" she snapped, as she stood to her feet with a deep scowl on her face.

"Nooo! He's not being seen," I said as I laughed at her. I watched the frown fade away and waited for the smile to return.

"Oh!" she said then sat back down.

"He's in the lobby. A girl he grew up with is also here and so is his little sister and me. They wouldn't let him come back here with me because they think he's going to roam the halls. Can you bring him back here?" I broke it down for her to understand.

I placed my hands together like I was pleading with her and batted my long eyelashes.

"What does he have on?" she asked after she laughed at me.

"I don't remember." I laughed as I tried hard to remember but couldn't. "Just yell Ray!" I said. I shocked myself with that one because I've never called him Ray before. I watched her nod her head and walk out of the room.

A few minutes later, Nurse Jennifer returned with a worried expression on her face as Rashard followed closely behind her. "What's the matter?" I asked with alarm evident in my voice.

"It's gonna be alright TT," Rashard said, as he took the nurse into a deep, loving embrace.

"TT?" I asked. I guess I was sitting here talking to my damn self the way they were carrying on and ignoring me.

"I'm about to go check on my baby. Call your mama and tell her to get her butt up here now!" she said and walked swiftly out of the room.

I waited patiently for him to finish the phone call that should have been placed to his mother the moment we pulled up with his little sister. When he ended the call, he looked stressed completely out. "Man, it's fina be some shit ma!" he said, as he ran his hands through his dreads.

"What's wrong?" I asked because if you ask me, the shit had already been handled.

"My mom, Janice, is a loose cannon when it comes down to us," he said and shook his head. He leaned back in the chair and slouched down. "I wasn't tryna call her because ain't shit she can do about shit but just be here. Anyway, how you feeling?" he asked. I knew that was his best attempt at changing the subject.

"I'm good, just ready to go home but nobody has been in here yet. We need to move Candy there until Deuce shows his lying face and can be there for her," I said all in one breath. I was really building up the courage to say what I really wanted to ask him. He looked at me with a weird expression like he already knew what I was about to ask him. I held my breath as I waited for him to respond.

"Why you call Deuce that?" he asked with his eyes squinting at me suspiciously.

"He hasn't been answering his phone for her, so I just figured something was up with him," I responded, as I stared him down.

He didn't respond and before I could dig any deeper, Dr. North came in the room to examine me. After she left, the x-ray tech came in with the x-ray machine and took x-rays of damn near my whole body, since everything was hurting. Hell, they would have been better off throwing me in the MRI machine but it's cool because I didn't want to have to lay still as long as you have to when you have one of those.

"How do you know my nurse?" I asked Rashard after everyone had come and gone out of my room.

"That's my mama sister," he said as he stood up. His phone was ringing and he was about to walk out of the door to answer it. All types of alarms started going off in my head and one thing I was not about to go through again was the shit I went through with Amere.

"Why you taking the call outside?" I asked, once he got to the door. I watched him nervously look between me and the screen on his phone, like he was weighing his options. He opened the door and left. I sat there trying to figure out what I was going to do. The house he bought me is beautiful but I don't want to build a home with someone I couldn't trust. At the same time, I can't go back to Candy's house with everything that happened there, even though Brandon is dead. I should just get my own place since I'm going to be working soon.

Lisa

After Michelle got dressed, we headed back to the living room to join the others. When we walked in, no one looked at us and it was probably because Michelle snaps out whenever someone is looking at her. I grabbed a chair from the table for her to sit in and placed it next to the spot where I was going to sit. "Iight Twan, the floor is yours," Andre said to Twan, once we were seated. I could feel the heat from Andre's glare on the side of my face but I refused to look at him.

I watched Twan stand to his feet and fix his clothing then walk in front of the television. "I'm skipping the introductions and small talk. Let's get straight to it," he paused and then looked around the room. It appeared that he had everyone's undivided attention. Well, everyone except Michelle. "Ya'll failing miserably at ya'll jobs!" Twan continued. I noticed Michelle's body stiffen and I think everybody else did too.

Twan reached for his gun, so I reached for Michelle. "Calm down. He has a gun," I whispered in her ear. Her shoulders slowly relaxed as she sat back against the chair. "Use your words," I said to her. Twan watched her intensely before he moved his hand away from where I'm sure his gun is.

"Dre, what's your progress?" Twan asked with his attention on Andre.

"Man, I been taking care of my bitch. She just lost her daughter and shit, so I ain't been doing shit but making sure she good," Andre said. Twan shot me a menacing look like it was my fault they hadn't been able to reach out and touch Rashard yet.

"What's your progress?" Michelle asked Twan. I looked at her because she did not sound like Michelle at all at this moment. She had a slight smirk on her face but her eyes were as black as coal. If you have ever seen soulless eyes before, then you know exactly what I see when I look at her right now.

"Bitch, don't question me! What's your fucking progress?!" Twan snapped.

Michelle stood to her feet so fast, the chair fell over. I reached out and grabbed her arm to stop her. "Get da fuck off me!" she yelled and snatched her arm away from me. Daphney and I both jumped on the other side of the couch when she looked in our direction. "STOP IT!!!" I heard Michelle scream. I peeked my head over the couch to look at her because she sounded like herself again.

I watched the color in her eyes come back slowly but I didn't move. "I'm sorry Lisa," she said, as she walked around the couch. I looked at her with fear written all over my face as I reached out and grabbed her extended hand, so she could help me stand up. I slowly walked back around the couch with her as I took a questioning gaze in Andre's direction. He shrugged his shoulders as I sat down on the couch. I watched Michelle pick her chair up and then sit down.

"I've been following Tamia. She got a new boo, Brandon," Michelle said but nobody responded. Everyone was looking at her, probably trying to figure out if they should respond or not.

"Ray got a few other chicks from what I heard. I have an inside man, well girl, Armani," she said and I could see a sparkle in Twan's eyes.

"Damn, good work!" Twan exclaimed. I could tell he was excited about her having someone on the inside. "Where's your cousin?" he asked, as if it had just dawned on him that someone was missing.

"Dead," Michelle answered like it was nothing.

From my understanding, they were joined at the hips so it'd be more like losing a sister rather than a cousin, but she doesn't care. "Who killed her?" Twan asked, like he was getting amped up.

"Me," she said with a shrug. I don't think there was a jaw in the room that wasn't on the floor when she said that.

"What?" she asked, like she really had no clue why everybody was looking at her with shocked expressions on their faces.

"Why'd you do it?" Twan asked.

"She had been sleeping with Rashard so she had to go," she said then stood to her feet. "Drive me home Lisa; my head hurts," Michelle said to me. I glanced over at Andre and could see the vein in his forehead protruding, which let me know he was upset.

"Come straight back!" he said through gritted teeth.

I didn't miss the shocked expression on Twan's face as I quickly nodded my head and followed Michelle out of the door.

"Aye wait!" I heard someone yell, as I was climbing into the driver's seat of Michelle's car. I looked towards the apartment buildings and saw Bo running towards me. "He probably need a ride," I said to Michelle, who sat in the passenger's seat with her attitude on 10! I swear, this girl's attitude is a force by itself.

"Why you let him do you like that?" he asked out of breath.

"That's none of your concern," I replied.

"Listen man, you deserve much better than that. I can see you've been through a lot and letting a nigga beat on you ain't gone make yo life easier," he said. The way he was looking at me, I could tell he has pity on my current predicament but I have a plan.

"I'm almost free," I said, as I looked up at the living room window. I could feel someone staring at me and lo and behold, the blinds are open. I'd bet my last dollar that Andre is seething with anger at this very moment.

"You might want to watch your back now," I said after I looked away from the window. Bo turned around and looked up to see what I was looking at.

"He don't want these problems. Listen, I can protect you," he said.

"Get in," I said, then hopped in the car.

"What are you doing?" Michelle asked. I glanced over at the blank expression on her face, which reminded me that I'm trying to play a lunatic.

"I need his help but I can't talk here," I said to her, as Bo climbed in the back seat. I quickly cranked the car up and drove off.

We rode in silence for about ten minutes, so I could gather my thoughts. Neither one of them said a word but the tension in the car was so thick, you could cut it with a knife. "You know you can trust me right," Bo began but the sound of Michelle sucking her teeth stopped him from talking. I looked over at her and could see her panting in her seat.

"Pull over!" she said. I glanced over at her like she was crazy because we are currently on the expressway.

"Mich-"

"PULL OVER!!" she screamed, grabbed the steering wheel, and snatched it in her direction. The car veered into another lane barely missing another car. I snatched the wheel back, attempting to regain control, but that only made everything worse. The entire car started to spin. I turned the wheel in the other direction in hopes of getting it back straight as I slammed on the brakes. The car continued to spin and began to tip slightly. Fear swept through my body as I let go of the wheel and removed my foot from the brake pedal.

All four tires were planted back on the road as the car slowed to a stop in the middle of the expressway. I breathed slow, deep breaths as I tried to slow my heart rate down. I looked at Michelle and Bo, and they both were breathing just as heavy as I was. *BEEEEEP!!!* The sound of a horn caught my attention and when I looked up, an 18 wheeler truck was headed straight for us.

Rashard

The hardest thing I have had to do in a long time was walk away from Tamia at a time when I know she needed me. In the short amount of time that we've been dating, I've grown to admire the strong woman that she is. All I want is to make sure she's happy but shit, I'm still trying to figure out how to balance all of the things I have going on in my life. Lately, I've been being pulled and stretched in every direction.

I haven't been to see my mama in a few weeks because I was trying to cover all bases. I know eventually she will meet Tamia, and I didn't want Tamia to mention me being in a coma because my mama will put me on blast. None of my family members knows about anything, other than Tamia. I know you may think I'm wrong but shit, I'm just trying to make everybody happy. The problem is, I may end up hurting everybody in the process. Hopefully, they'll understand what I've been going through.

Then, there's my empire. I've been neglecting it too for the past few weeks and the streets were damn near dry until some cat from out of town started supplying them. I'm not worried about him though because my shit is exclusive and from what I hear, his shit is watered down. With that being said, when I send my people that **I'm in need** text, it will take no time for everything to flood the streets. The good thing about what I do is, people can be gunning for my position but they have no idea who I am, so they could never stop anything on my end.

On top of that, Chardae has been texting and calling me since I been at the hospital. At first, I knew she was just in her feelings about what I said to her and how I left her, but now she's on some dumb shit. The text she sent me right before my aunt Jennifer came in the lobby to get me said she wasn't going to allow me to see my son. I didn't respond to her because I got distracted with my aunt and I wanted to wait until she gave me an update on my sister.

When Tamia asked me why I was leaving to take the call, my first thought was to just come clean about the baby because I didn't want to keep lying to her. That's why I just left. I'll be back to check on her, Myra, and Candy but I needed to do some mending to ensure that I could be a part of my son's life.

I halfway expected Tamia to start yelling and cursing but she did none of that. She didn't call out to me as I walked out of the door and I hoped like hell she wasn't already done with a nigga. I know the cupcake phase of our relationship hasn't even been a cupcake phase but if she just be patient and let me get shit together on my end, it will all get better.

"Where you goin?" I heard my Aunt Jennifer ask from behind me.

"Fina get Tamia something from the store," I responded then turned around to face her. She was looking at me like she knew I was lying but she didn't say anything. "How's Myra?" I asked.

"She's going to be alright. She has a few broken ribs and a few bruised ones. They have her heavily sedated at my request, so she won't feel any pain. I plan on keeping her here for as long as I can, so she can rest and heal," she explained. "So, you will have to help your mom out with the baby," she continued.

If Tamia hadn't already killed Brandon, I would have been heading in his direction to torture him slowly. I nodded my head and turned to walk away when she grabbed my hand. "That's a really good girl in there. Don't lose her. You won't find her again," she said and walked away.

"Fuck!" I said out loud to myself as I walked in the lobby of the ER.

"You leaving?" Armani asked. I shot her a look and she looked away. This bitch has been a pain in my ass for too damn long. If she keeps on with the bullshit, she will be sleeping with the fish.

My phone chimed, indicating I had a text message.

Natasia: i wanna feel u

I could feel my dick getting hard, so I readjusted myself in my pants. Ok, yea, I know I ain't shit but that damn Natasia can do some things with her mouth piece and the way she throws that ass back, I haven't been able to leave her alone. All she had to do was send a text like this one or one of those random freaky pictures and I was on my way. She knew what she had and she knew exactly how to use it, and I took full advantage of it. The bright side of that is, Natasia knows her position and she plays it well. Well shit, I haven't given her a reason to act up, so I hope she remains cool, calm, and collect this dick.

"Which one are you going to see?" I heard Armani ask once I made it to my car. I turned around to face her with a scowl on my face until I realized she was looking at my dick.

"Bitch, mind ya damn business and stop looking at my dick," I said as I hopped in the car.

"You gone give it to me one way or another," she said and walked off. I watched her walk all the way back inside the ER. Her ass jiggled with each step she took. I sat there in a daze until my phone started ringing.

"I'm on my way," I said then disconnected the call. When I pulled up to her house, she was already standing in the doorway. I got pissed off because she never has on clothes when she opens the door. "Get yo gahdamn ass in da house girl!" I snapped as I slammed the door to my car. She had on one of my muscle shirts and that looked like all she had on.

"Where you been?" she asked, as she placed her small hand on her thick hip. I could see her pregnant belly slightly and smiled as I approached her. "Where have you been?!" she yelled.

"You need to calm down because you're putting that stress on my baby," I said, as I rubbed her stomach. I felt the tension leave her body and I just don't understand why she let me have so much control over her feelings. When I was here, I was spitting real shit at her, so I hoped she was listening.

I sat down on the couch and pulled her down next to me, so I could rub her stomach. She reached for my zipper but I swatted her hand away. She frowned up at me instantly and I could see she was fighting back tears. This pregnancy is really taking an emotional toll on her. "Chill out with the tears Chardae, do we need to talk again?" I asked because I needed us to be on the same page. I'm not fucking her no more because she's confusing the shit and thinking I want to be with her, and that's probably my fault because I fuck her like I love her.

"Why are you doing this to me?" she asked, as she laid her head on my chest. I wanted to move her off of me because she was already getting shit twisted but I needed to calm her down.

"I'm not doing nothing. Well, I'm not trying to," I responded to her. I could tell that we were about to have a long conversation and I'm not leaving here until we have an understanding.

"You love me, right?" she asked, as she looked up at me.

"As the mother of my child, yes. I'll always make sure you're straight because if you're straight, then he's straight," I said. I was trying my best to break it down for her, so she would understand and her feelings wouldn't be hurt.

"Why don't you want to be with me? Like, give our family a shot," she asked and it irritated the fuck out of me. I scooted away from her and made her face me.

"Chardae, I didn't try to have a baby with you but it happened. I'm going to take care of you both but I'm not going to be with you," I said, clearly frustrated. I tried to take a few deep breaths to calm down before I snapped out on her for begging me to be with her.

"Why not?" she asked. I read her facial expression and she looked calm like she was ready for this conversation.

"I'm with someone already. That's who I'm going to be with," I said and her eyes damn near bugged out of her head.

"When did this happen because the last few weeks, you been with me every day!" she snapped and I could tell she was pissed off.

"Think about it for a second. Have I been here or do I just come over when you need something? Being here and being here for you are two different things. I'll always be here for you because of him," I said, then pointed at her stomach. She shook her head and stood up but I pulled her back down.

"Get all of your questions out, so you can get whatever you need to get out and over with because we're not doing this again," I said to her. She frowned up at me, like I was wrong when I was only trying to help.

"Who's going to be around my child and what she got going for herself?" she asked, as she sat back and crossed her arms over her chest.

"Her name is Tamia. She just graduated from UMA with me and will be working at the hospital. Trust me like I'm going to trust you that no harm will come to him while he's with us," I said to her. The look she gave me made me think she understood where I was coming from.

"Why her?" she asked and shock filled my face.

"What you mean?" I asked, once her question registered.

"Why her and not me?" she asked. I didn't come here to belittle her and I don't want to make her feel like shit by going through the list of qualities that Tamia possess that she doesn't. Hell, I haven't even fucked Tamia yet and she got me in the process of cutting bitches off. I done already bought her a house so we can build together. I'm sure ya'll think I'm moving too fast but I done already had everybody, and I've never met anyone even remotely similar to Tamia. I know I ain't shit but I know when I've snagged a good one.

My phone chimed and all I could think was "Saved by the bell". I checked to see what it was and it was that **It's a go message** from one of my runners. Since I got that one, I knew I needed to head out and get the money to drop off before the rest of my runners were ready. "Call me later so we can go get the baby some stuff from the mall. I have to go check on my sister," I said, as I stood up.

"He don't need anything right now," she said with a slight attitude. I could tell she was frustrated but she will have to get over it.

I shook my head and headed out the door. I felt like someone was watching me, so I quickly checked my surroundings and didn't see anything out of place. *If someone is here then they will surely stand out in this neighborhood,* I thought to myself as I continued to walk to my car. I opened the door and opened one of the secret compartments and got a .45 out of it. I concealed it and walked back inside. I needed to give Chardae the gun, in case someone is lurking and run in there on her.

"Yea... He just left... Shit, iono, just follow him and get it! ...Aw fuck, do I have to do everything! Ok Joe, I'm sorry, just don't lose him... I know... Love you too." I stood in the foyer shocked as I listened to Chardae's one sided conversation.

Michelle

I regretted snatching the wheel the moment I did it. I regretted it even more as we sat idly in the middle of the expressway with an 18 wheeler heading straight for us. I clenched my shirt over my chest as I tried desperately to brace myself for the impact. I watched the truck get closer and closer and all I could think about was not killing Tamia before I died.

All of sudden, the car took off with so much force that my head jerked backwards and hit the seat. At the same time, the truck driver switched lanes and ran a Ford Explorer off the road. I watched in horror as the Ford Explorer flipped three times then collided with a small two door Honda. I got on my knees in my seat as we pulled off and left the scene, so I could watch the wreckage. It had reached a 6 car pileup, not including the 18 wheeler truck. I shook my head and turned around and sat down.

"Find somewhere to pull over," I stated calmly.

"Ok," Lisa said and it shocked me. I just knew she was going to give me some lip about the accident I caused but nobody said a word. At least not until we got off at the next exit and parked at a gas station.

"What the fuck is yo problem man? You could have gotten us killed!" Bo snapped at me. My eyes got huge as I had a flashback of this same man beating me halfway to death.

"Do you not remember almost killing me?! Or was I supposed to forget? You beat da fuck outta me and now I hear voices! I'm gonna kill you, Bo. I told her to pull over to give you a head start because when I catch you, I'm gonna kill you! Get da fuck out my car!!!" I screamed at the top of my lungs.

I'm pretty sure people were looking at me crazy but I didn't give a mammy fat fuck! Shit, he's lucky that I don't have a knife in my car or I would have killed him already. "Chelle, I'm sorry about that. Lemme explain please?" he pleaded. I glanced over at Lisa and could see the tears in her eyes and knew, she's indeed my friend. My pain is now her pain.

"Get out Bo." she said calmly without looking back. Bo looked at me then her, shook his head, and climbed out of the car.

Lisa pulled off before the door was closed good. "I'm sorry Michelle. I didn't know," she said somberly, as she shook her head. I nodded my forgiveness as I turned around and buckled my seatbelt. I gave her directions to my house, so we could go in and catch up. I needed to know everything about her if we're going to be friends.

*** Back at Michelle's House ***

"I can't believe that bitch was sleeping with your man!" I said after Lisa told me that Tamia took Amere from her. That scandalous bitch just goes around taking everybody's man. She told me Tamia moved here to get away from Amere because once he found out Lisa was pregnant, he left Tamia. Then they started messing around again and he tricked Lisa into moving here, so he could get back with Tamia! That bitch is trifling! Ray has no idea who he thinks he's in love with.

"We should expose her for the hoe she is!" I said with my voice laced with excitement.

"We have to take care of these men first," she said, which caught me off guard because I don't even have a man.

"What you mean?" I asked her.

"I'm not gonna be safe until Andre is dead but I don't know how to kill anyone; can you help me?" she asked with tears in her eyes. I nodded my head and she jumped up and hugged me. "Now, we have to kill Bo too because you threatened him, so now he's gonna try to kill you first," she said and I felt so stupid.

I know you're not supposed to threaten anyone and let them walk away. That's like pulling a gun out on someone and not pulling the trigger. "Who do we kill first?" I asked her. It felt good to talk to someone that let me help make decisions versus when the voices demand that I do something.

"Bo," she said and I nodded my head.

We sat around watching TV until it got dark. I threw on a black jogging suit and used gel to slick my short hair down over my head. I gave Lisa a brown jogging suit to put on and she threw her hair in a short ponytail. She's skinny like me so it fit around the waist but since she's taller than me, the pants weren't long enough for her. I gave her some tennis shoes and we were out the door.

We climbed in my car, but this time, I'm driving because I know exactly where we're going. "What's in the bag?" Lisa asked, as we pulled out of my apartment complex.

"Knives. You gotta figure out which one you like to kill with," I answered and she nodded her head. I continued to drive until I pulled up to Rashard's mom's house.

I'd heard through the grapevine that Bo had moved back home with their mother. I stopped in front of their house and cut the car off. "Wait," Lisa said, as I opened the car door.

"What?" I asked, hoping she wasn't about to punk out.

"You can't park here. What if someone recognizes your car? Go down there somewhere," she explained. I smiled as I took another look at the house and parked a few house down.

We walked casually on the sidewalk, so we wouldn't look suspicious. Once we were back in front of Ray's mom's house, I removed the backpack and got my butcher's knife out for me. Lisa's eyes grew big but I couldn't tell if she was afraid or excited. I handed her the backpack, so she could get a knife out of it. I laughed softly at the knife she chose. "What's funny?" she asked, clearly confused.

"What you gone do with that small ass knife?" I asked, as I continued to laugh at her. She shrugged her shoulders and sat the bag down on the sidewalk.

I led the way to the house. Back when I use to come over here, Ms. Janice would complain about a window in the back of the house that wouldn't lock. I crossed my fingers with hope that she hadn't gotten it fixed. "Stay low," I said to Lisa, even though the house was pitch dark, except for one room. Hopefully, for Rashard's sake, his mom isn't here because she was always a nice lady and I'd hate to have to kill her.

We made it to the window and it was still unlocked. I opened it with ease and slid my slim body inside the house. I waited patiently for Lisa to do the same. "Well, wake up the neighbors while you're at it," I said sarcastically because of all the noise she was making as she climbed in the window behind me.

"Well, this isn't something I do every day, ya know," she said, as she rolled her eyes. She fell down as soon as she made it inside of the room we were in.

"Shit girl! We should have just knocked on the fucking door!" I said, as I popped her in the back of the head.

I helped her to her feet and watched her fix her clothes then rub the spot that I hit her in. When she removed her hand, it had blood on it. "Fuck Michelle, what you hit me with?" she asked, as she touched the spot again and got more blood on her hand. I looked in my hand and noticed there was blood on my knife.

"I'm sorry Lisa," I said and showed her the blood on the knife.

She shook her head at me as she grimaced in pain. "Well, get over it; at least you're still alive," I whispered harshly.

"I knew you would come but I didn't know you would come so soon," I heard Bo say, then the flights flickered on. He stood in the doorway with a gun in his hands and we're standing here with knives in ours.

Talk about bringing a knife to a gunfight, I thought to myself as I stared at Bo. He had this evil grin on his face as he looked at me.

"Ya know, I'd like to sample that pussy again before I kill you Michelle," he said, as he licked his lips. He walked closer to me and I looked over at Lisa. She had blood dripping down her back as she swayed from side to side.

"Mi… Mich… Michelle," Lisa said as she reached around her, trying to grab something to keep from falling.

I reached for her but Bo pulled me away from her and towards him. I tried to stab him but he grabbed my wrist and squeezed it tightly until I let go of the knife. Lisa hit the floor, so I had no help. I looked up into Bo's menacing eyes as he rubbed all over my body. He had the gun pressed firmly against my side as he squeezed my breasts.

"Aww, don't cry," he said, as he wiped the tears away as they fell from my eyes. He jerked my pants down and ripped my panties off. He snatched them so hard that the material nicked some of my skin off. I didn't move or try to fight him off as he placed a finger inside of me. I tried to fight back the tears as I stood there as stiff as a board.

"Why are you letting him do this?!" I heard the voice scream out.

"Kill him dummy!" she screamed.

"I can't!!!" I cried out because I didn't know what to do.

Tamia

I laid in the hospital bed trying to figure out if I should break up with him based solely off of an assumption or stick it out and see what happens. Nurse Jennifer has been in and out of all of our rooms to check on us since Rashard left, and that was well over an hour ago. His mom is here but she's in the room with Myra and as sad as it may sound, I'm glad I don't have to meet her. Especially since her daughter is here because of me. I should have listened to Candy and not given Brandon a chance, and neither one of us would be in the ER right now at all. I shook my head as I reflected on the first sign I had that Brandon was crazy.

I had just gotten in from work. I went to my room and grabbed some clothes, so I could take a shower when my phone started to ring. I walked over to my bed where the phone was and saw that it was Brandon calling. "I'll call him back after my shower," I thought to myself. I walked back over to the dresser and allowed the phone to continue to ring as I grabbed my underwear out of my drawer.

I took a shower and a few seconds after I entered my room, my phone started ringing again. I smiled to myself when I noticed it was Brandon calling back. "I'll call him once I get dressed," I said out loud to myself as I began to lotion my skin. I got dressed and brushed my wet hair up into a messy bun. I grabbed my kindle and climbed on the bed. As soon as I got good into the book I was reading, my phone chimed, indicating I had a text message:

Brandon: *I just wantd 2 c how ur day was bt i c ur screenin my calls*

"No, it couldn't have been," I said, as I sat completely up in the hospital bed. I winced in pain but I got to see if I'm wrong. I pulled the covers back and swung my legs off the bed.

"What are you doing?" Nurse Jennifer asked, as she walked in my room and saw me trying to get out of bed.

"I need to get home," I said, as my skin began to itch.

I could feel the lump forming in my throat as I looked at the confused face in front of me. "Sweetie, you can't leave until you have been cleared. Wait until Rashard comes back and get him to do whatever you need him to do," she said, all the while laying me back down on the bed and covering my body.

Even with the sheet over me, I felt exposed. I pulled it up around my neck as I looked around the room. I tried to focus my thoughts on something else but all I could think about is, what if I had a camera in my room? My mind flashed back to a phone conversation we had.

I was doing squats in my room when my phone rang. It was the first day I hadn't gotten a chance to speak with Brandon since we started conversing, so I knew it was him. "Hello sir," I said, as I smiled into the phone.

"Hey yourself. You're breathing heavy; you must have been working out?" he asked.

"Yep!" I said, as I tried to slow my breathing. I heard him chuckle softly.

"Let me guess, squats?" he asked. I furrowed up my eyebrows after he said that.

"How you know?" I asked him cautiously.

"That's all females ever do," he answered.

"Oh!" I said, as I wiped the sweat off of my forehead.

"What you thought, I planted cameras in your room and was watching you or something?" he asked with a laughed.

"No," I said, as I laughed nervously.

"What's the matter Tamia?" Nurse Jennifer asked. Her question snapped me out of my thoughts.

"I think... I think he was recording me," I said with tears falling freely down my cheeks.

"Who?" she asked, after she closed the door completely.

"Brandon, this guy I was dating," I answered her after she pulled the chair closer to my bed.

"Wait, I thought you were dating Rashard," she said with a confused expression on her face, accompanied with a slight frown. "I was but we weren't official. After he slipped into a coma, I conversed with Brandon," I explained but the frown got deeper.

"Tamia, who slipped in a coma?" she asked and all types of alarms started ringing in my head as I began to get lost in my thoughts again.

I got off early because we were slow and parked my car in the garage that Candy never uses. She said she doesn't use it because sometimes it sticks, and she's late so much that fighting with the garage door would just cause more problems. I walked in through the garage door that led into the kitchen. I walked around the house but Candy wasn't home. You never knew when she was here because sometimes she'd get wasted at work and need to be dropped off, so her car wouldn't be here. Then, sometimes, she just didn't feel like driving and would call one of the girls to come get her and her car would be here.

After I didn't find her, I went to my room to wash the hospital's smell off of my body. I cut the shower off and heard the front door open, followed by Candy's loud voice. The only time she uses her inside voice is when she's around someone else. I dried my body off then lotioned it up. I threw on some sweatpants and a t-shirt, so I could go find Candy and vent about my long work day.

"Yea, well I'll be happy when you're ready to be a man... Fuck all that... Ok, sleeping beauty, whatever." I heard her one sided conversation as I walked down the hall and into her room. As soon as I walked through the door, she dropped her phone. "Bitch you scared the entire fuck out of me!" she said as she snatched the phone off the floor. She hung it up without telling them bye. I frowned at her. "Niggas," she said with a shrug of the shoulders and that explained it all for me.

"She knew," I said out loud to myself.

"Who knew what sweetie?" Jennifer asked and for a minute, I forgot she was there.

"Fuck my life!" I said exasperated. I've never been able to trust anybody and right when I'm ready to open myself up again, it proves that it's safer not to trust anybody.

"What's going on sweetie? I'm lost," Jennifer asked.

"I'm going to separate myself from everybody. I'm going to work my butt off here and you won't regret your decision of hiring me. I want to be moved to another room and I want to be made confidential, so nobody knows where I am," I said and she looked even more confused than she did before. I bet she thinks I'm crazy right now but at this moment, I don't even trust her. I'll figure out my living arrangements once I'm discharged.

"Ok," she said, as she stood to her feet. She had no choice but to honor my confidential request and by law, she wouldn't be able to tell Rashard or anyone else where I am. Well, she could, but she would lose her job in the process.

I figured I'd deal with Armani once I'm released because right now, I just don't have the energy to deal with anyone. Especially sketchy people! Hell, I wouldn't be surprised if she was somewhere fucking Rashard right now or trying to.

Missy

"STOP!" I screamed and head butted the fuck out of Bo. I've been trying to protect Michelle for as long as I can remember. She use to let me out more often whenever she was faced with situations she couldn't handle. Then she met her precious Rashard and blocked me out! She couldn't even hear me telling her what to do anymore. It wasn't until Bo came and beat her unconscious that she lost self-control. She's been giving up slowly and after we killed Tiffany, she's been unable to control when I come out. In this moment, she needs me more than ever and I won't let her down.

I looked at Bo with a smile on my face. He had blood dripping from his nose and the veins in his neck were protruding. He swung a closed fist at me but I expected that and ducked just in time. I grabbed the lamp off of the desk and hit him over the head with it. It shattered but did nothing to slow him down. He charged at me but I rolled my small frame under the desk, and he ended up hitting it. The entire desk flipped over, so I took that chance to look for another weapon. The only thing I saw was the sewing machine but it looked too heavy to use during a counter attack.

Right when I wanted to give up, I saw a shimmer of light. I looked on the floor to my left and noticed the street light reflected off of the knife Michelle dropped minutes ago. I dove for it but not before I received a swift kick to my stomach. It sent me flying in the air until I hit the tree in the back of the room. "Fuck!" I said out loud, as I touched my stomach. It was already tender to the touch, so I knew the bruise would be something serious.

Before I had time to get up, Bo was on top of me with his hands wrapped tightly around my throat. He was slamming my body against the floor over and over as I tried to scratch and claw at his face. I began to feel dizzy and faint, like I was losing consciousness. I fought harder and swung my arms wildly. "Just give up," I heard Michelle's voice say. I started bucking my body in an attempt to throw him off of me but nothing worked. "Just give up," she said again.

"SHUT... UP!" I managed to scream out. I didn't miss the confused look Bo gave me, then his eyes turned dark. I stopped fighting because my best way out was to pretend to give in. I could feel my powerful energy fade back in as the fight left my body. "No I can't," I heard her plead.

I looked past Bo and saw Lisa's dumb ass finally getting up, and that's all I needed to stay in the game. I stared off in the distance as Bo kept one hand planted firmly around my throat as he fumbled with his belt buckle with his free hand. I knew exactly what he was about to do to me and there was nothing I could do about it. He pulled his pants and boxers down and began to beat his meat until it got hard.

It wasn't getting hard for him, so he spit in his hand and jerked it faster. I watched it grow and fear filled my body. I don't know what's going to happen to Michelle if I allow him to do this. He raised off of me slightly, so he could part my legs. He was so busy trying to get his dick hard enough to rape me that he had released the grip he had on my throat. He had been slowly sliding his hand away from my neck. I was lying perfectly still as I waited for the perfect moment to attack.

I looked past him again and Lisa still wasn't completely up. Maybe she was never really out and was just too weak to help me out. I looked back at Bo because he was now fully erect. I couldn't figure out why Lisa wasn't helping me. I focused my thoughts on killing her after I killed him.

"Mmmhh," Bo moaned out in pleasure as he forced himself inside of me. I tuned him out completely as I watched Lisa. The insides of my pussy burned as he ripped through. I winced in pain and I could feel the wetness start to slide down to my butt. The pain subsided but it didn't feel good as he continued to hump away inside of me.

I continued to watch Lisa flutter her eyes. I think she thought that I didn't know she was awake as she lay still on the floor while I got raped a few steps away from her. "You missed this dick, didn't you?" Bo asked, as he turned my head so I was forced to look at him. I nodded my head as tears of anger and rage seeped from eyes. "Why you crying then bitch?" he asked, as he rammed his dick in me harder and harder.

"I wanna switch," I said, as I tried my hardest to sound seductive. I failed miserably at seduction because it came out hoarse. He smiled at me and gripped my breast with his free hand. "Ok, get on top but don't try no slick shit, or I'm gonna choke the shit outta you!" he snapped.

He gripped my neck tighter as he rotated his body while his dick was still inside of me. I adjusted my body once I was on top, so it wouldn't hurt so bad. I started to ride him slowly and he moaned out. I rose all the way to the head and slammed down on top of him. He closed his eyes, so I did it again. I could see the knife and it wasn't far away. I slowed my pace, so he wouldn't cum before I grabbed the knife.

I glanced over at the spot we were just in and saw blood on the floor. I got pissed off completely. I looked at him with pure disgust written all over my face as I gained control of my rape. I rotated my hips as I rode him slowly, so he would close his eyes. I began to grind on him with his dick deep inside of me.

I reached as far as I could and he opened his eyes. I moaned out to distract him from what I was doing. He pushed me back up so I could ride him how I was at first, as he unzipped the jacket that goes with my jogging suit. He moaned as I leaned forward and began to grind against him again. He lifted my shirt and took a nipple into his mouth. "Oooh shit!" Michelle moaned and threw me for a complete loop. This shit ain't supposed to be pleasurable to her but she's enjoying it.

Bo got good dick, without a doubt, but he has to die for sticking it where it wasn't welcomed. I released a breath I didn't know I was holding, once I was able to grab the knife. I felt a joy like no other as I gripped the knife tightly and held it behind my back. "Damn baby, you getting wetter now!" Bo said. I smiled because he thought I was getting wet because of him, but the truth is, I cum when I kill.

I raised the knife above my head as I rode him slowly and brought the knife down into his chest. He gasped for air and punched me so hard that I flew off of him. He tried to pull the knife out but it was stuck. He turned over on his side and spit blood out on the floor. "You killed... you killed our baby," Bo choked out. "Now, you gonna kill me," he continued. I stood up so I could step on the knife and kill him when I heard sirens in the distance.

"What the fuck!" I screamed at the top of my lungs. I quickly slipped my pants back on and grabbed my ripped panties. I looked over at Lisa and she still had her eyes closed, like she didn't hear the damn sirens. I guess she wasn't pretending to be out. I ran out the front door and down the steps. I grabbed my backpack off the sidewalk and walked casually down the street to my car. I let the seat all the way back as the police flew past me and stopped abruptly in front of Bo's mom's house. "Nosey ass neighbors must have saw us climbing through the window," I said out loud, as I cranked the car up and drove home.

Rashard

I waited patiently for Chardae to get off the phone, so I could kill her. When I heard her end the call, I made my way to where she was. The dummy didn't even get up to make sure I was gone before she told a mufucker about my departure. I shook my head and walked completely in the living room where I left the dumb duck.

"Oh shit! What you doing here?" she said and dropped her phone. She had fear written all over her face, like she'd just seen a ghost.

"What you mean?" I asked, as I took a step closer to her. Her body tensed up and she slid to the other side of the couch. "What's your problem?" I asked her, as I sat down next to her on the couch.

I placed my hand on her stomach and felt the baby inside of it kick. I no longer believe this is my kid. She played me and if she wasn't pregnant, she'd be dead already. "You don't want me here?" I asked, as I leaned into her. I put my nose in the crook of her neck and inhaled her sweet scent. Her body relaxed and she melted in my arms.

"Yea but I thought you were going to check on your sister," she said, as she threw her arm around my neck and started playing with my dreads.

"I am but I wanted to make sure you were straight before I left," I said and looked up at her. She was smiling and I knew it was because she thought she got over on me. I smiled back because she hadn't.

"I'll catch you later," I said, as I stood to my feet.

"Where is your sister?" she asked.

"Why?" I countered.

"Oh! Just asking. I thought you were gonna go do more than check on her," she said and it let me know what I heard about her after I first started fucking her was true.

I was sitting at the bar inside of Carte Blanche, a year or so after it opened, when Chardae came in with her girls. She caught my eye as soon as she walked through the doors and I knew I had to have her. When I walked up to her, she didn't play hard to get or nothing and that turned me on more than anything. When I looked at her, I saw a woman who knew what she wanted and wasn't afraid to ask for it. We were in a VIP booth fucking before the night was over and been straight fucking ever since.

About 3 months later, Raph came up to me and asked if I was still messing with her. I looked at him crazy and asked him why. "She a stripper down at the Foxy Lady. Not just a stripper though, she got this dude that she helps set niggas up to get robbed," Raph explained. I don't go off hearsay and I wasn't getting any bad vibes from her.

After that, I started going to the Foxy Lady every Friday night and every other Saturday night to see if I would run into her, and I never did. That reason, and that reason alone, is why I wrote off what Raph said me.

I backed out of Chardae's temporary driveway and pulled off. I called it a temporary driveway because as soon as I found the nigga she was working with and killed him, she was getting her walking papers.

When I got to the stop sign on the corner, I noticed a little, old ass raggedy car with a dark skinned dude driving. I pulled off slowly and his dumb ass didn't even stop at the sign, so he could keep up with me. I pulled out my phone and called Twan, so we could set up a trap but he didn't answer his phone. I hit end and called Dre, and he didn't answer either.

"What the fuck?" I said out loud, as I looked in my rearview mirror and saw buddy was still following me. I knew I couldn't call Deuce after how our last conversation, so I called Tre. "What up Boss?" he asked and I laughed. Candy's ass is rubbing off on everybody.

"Ay, where you at?" I asked, once I stopped laughing.

"The dungeon," he answered.

"Alright, check this out. A bih is trying to set me up and I got buddy following me now," I spoke clearly into the receiver.

"Lead him here. We got you," he said and disconnected the call.

One thing I've always noticed about Tre and Deuce was they have never let me down. They always have my back, even though when I started school, I linked up with Twan and Dre. Deuce use to tell me all the time he didn't trust Twan and that Dre wasn't ready for this life. I never listened but the deeper I get in this shit, the less I can count on them niggas.

I took a right, so I could circle around and head to the dungeon. They call it the dungeon because it's our only trap house that only has one way in and out. The only way you can get in is through the front door, unless you break a window. They don't have to worry about the police because it takes them a few hours to come pick up a dead body. Plus, there's only one way on and off the block by car. Now, if you're on foot, you can cut in between buildings but in the car, you can only drive out the way you drove in because it's a dead end.

When I got ready to turn in, I checked the rearview mirror and watched him drive past. I kept my eyes trained on his car until I saw the brake lights come. I waved Peanut over, so I could holla at him. I've been knowing Peanut since he was eight years old and he was the lookout for Tre. Now, his little ass is sixteen, and every day after school and on the weekends, he gets on the roof and knocks people off with his sniper rifle.

"What's up Shard?" he asked, as he dapped me up.

"Aye, you saw that beat up car that was following me but just past by?" I asked. He nodded his head without looking for the vehicle. See, Peanut is smart and he's loyal. Anybody else his age, I would have had to tell them not to look for it because it would let him know we're on to him.

"This bih tryna set me up. Let him in alive but he won't leave the same way," I said with a straight face.

"Bet," he responded and turned to walk away.

"Aye Shard!" Peanut yelled after I pulled off.

"Yea?" I answered him.

"Congratulations man. I'm tryna be like you!" he said with a smile. I knew he was showing love about me graduating college. "Don't be like me Nut. Be better than me," I said and pulled off. The last thing I want is for a kid to want to be like me at this point in my life. Never strive to be like someone else; it's so much easier to just be yourself. Figure out what it is that you're good at and be great at it. Set goals and accomplish them. Compete only with the person that you were yesterday. If more people was like that, then the world would be a much more productive place.

I drove all the way to end of the street and hopped out of my car. I didn't know which trap Tre was in, so I looked at every lower leveled window until I saw him. The blinds weren't open but I knew he would be looking out of one of them, so I headed in that direction.

When I walked on the porch, I saw buddy pull in slowly, like he was looking for me. I turned to walk back to my car. "What you doing?" Tre asked, after he swung the door open. I signaled for him to give me one moment. I grabbed my school book bag out of the backseat and carried it up to the door. I watched the car come to a stop with my peripheral vision just a few houses over. I looked around like I had a bag filled with either money or dope and walked in the house.

"Who set you up?" Tre asked, as I looked out the window.

"Bitch name Chardae that use to live in Dead Man's Cove," I answered.

"Man, I heard you was messing with that bitch! Man, that hoe set ya boy Darius up, and they got him for four keys and $100,000 cash!" Tre exclaimed, as he looked out the window. "He must gone wait til you bout to leave to get at u," Tre continued, without giving me a chance to respond to his first comment.

"Man, is that why Herrar killed him?" I asked, as I shook my head.

A while back, Darius was one of my runners that would get coke from one of my connects, Herrar. I didn't even know he had gotten set up. All I know is he was killed, and his hands were cut off and delivered to his mother's front door. It had a note attached to the box they were delivered in that said "For those who take but did not earn, must pay dearly in their turn." I remember when I first read the note; I knew it sounded familiar. See, Myra is a huge Harry Potter fan and one of the characters on the sorcerer's stone said that. I didn't know until I said it in front of her and she asked if I had been watching Harry Potter without her. Thinking of that made me think about how she's doing and how pissed off she will be if I'm not there with her when she wakes up. After I handle this, I'm going back to the hospital to see what's up with my girls.

"Aye bruh, he getting out and he packin," Tre said calmly, like the fact that this nigga had a gun and was heading in our direction didn't bother him at all. I looked out the window and my mouth dropped. I expected him to get out with a pistol but this nigga had an Agram 200 machine gun with an extended clip.

"Man, this nigga ain't gone ever run outta bullets!" I said, hyped up.

My phone started ringing and when I pulled it out to check it, it was my aunt Jennifer. She wouldn't call me unless something was wrong. "Aye, call Peanut and tell him to take him out. I gotta go," I said to Tre. He grabbed his Boost mobile phone and chirped Peanut.

"Bet," Peanut chirped back. I looked through the blinds and watched buddy until he got in the yard. I swung the door opened and smiled at him. He had a confused look on his face as I walked outside.

"Who are you?" I asked, as I stepped off the porch.

"Yo worst nightmare," he said, as he aimed his machine gun at me. "Give it up and you'll live." he said calmly.

"Nigga, you fina die," I said to him.

"Nigga, Joe don't die!" he yelled before squeezing the trigger. I dove face first into the ground and rolled until the bullets stopped. My heart was pounding in my chest as I rolled over on my back and checked myself for any bullet holes.

"You good bruh?" Tre yelled from the door.

"Yea," I said, as I sat up and looked around. I looked down the street and saw Peanut hauling ass this way. I stood up and walked over to buddy and searched his pockets. "Nigga got a trap phone," I said, as I stuck it in my pocket. He didn't have any money in his wallet and his name was Joe Buck.

"My bad bruh, my rifle jammed," Peanut said, once he got within earshot and wouldn't have to yell.

"It's all good," I said because I shouldn't have brought my ass out here, like he ain't have a damn machine gun in his hands. "What's funny?" I asked Peanut because he was standing next to Joe's body laughing.

"Half this nigga's head gone," he said, as he bent over laughing.

I shook my head as I headed towards my car. "I appreciate that, my niggas. Call the cleanup crew," I said and drove off to check on my people.

Armani

I walked coolly back into the ER waiting area, trying to figure out if I tried my hand with Rashard too early or not. Thinking about it now, I probably should have waited until I was in Tamia's good graces again. I know she's talking to me and we were around each other today, but I also know that once you cross her, it's hard to get close to her again; if she ever lets you near her period. The fact that she's talking to me at all lets me know that there's hope.

Now, with Rashard, I know some shit about him that I know he doesn't want Tamia to know, so I can easily get the dick once we all move in together. See, I have to speak it into existence! I learned at church when I was younger that the power of the tongue is real. Speak positive things into your future and positive things will come. With that being said, if I speak this into my future, it too shall come to pass.

I sat around looking stupid as I wondered why Tamia hadn't sent for me to come be with her in her time of need. When she first went to the back, I figured she just wanted to be alone until that lady came out and got Rashard. Now that he's gone, you would think that she would want me back there with her.

I waited patiently for as long as I could before I decided to ask if I could go back. The girl at the window gave me her room number and opened the doors for me to enter. When I rounded the corner, she was being wheeled down the hallway by the same nurse that came out to get Rashard. I didn't yell out to them or anything; I just followed behind them. It looked like they were just moving her to another room.

"I'm not sure what's going on but I think you should talk with them all first and get a clear understanding because you could just be confused," I heard the lady say to Tamia. I stood outside of the room door, so I could eavesdrop on their conversation.

"They've been lying to me. I've had enough of people lying to me," Tamia said in her normal bratty tone. I bet she was sitting in the bed with her arms folded and everything.

"What are you going to do about a place to stay?" the lady asked, and my ears perked up at the thought of hearing about my new living arrangements. I'd live anywhere as long as I didn't have to go back to Joe.

"I don't know yet. I need to move out of Candy's house and get my own. Rashard bought us a house but I don't want to be around neither one of them," she stated and shocked the fuck out of me.

It may be easier than I thought to do everything I want to do to destroy her once and for all without killing her. If she separates herself from Candy, then she will be lonely any damn way and will need me as a friend to keep her sane. All I'll have to do is remind her of the good ole days before she started thinking that she was better than me. As for fucking Rashard, all I have to do is threaten to tell her about the fat chick he got put up in a nice house and the cute chick that he been fucking too. I can use that to blackmail him and make her think that I'm trying to get them to get back together.

Thoughts of Amere began to float around my head as I remembered him being here in this very hospital. *I need a plan b, in case Tamia doesn't let me live with her,* I thought to myself. I looked at the door to make sure I remembered Tamia's room number and headed back out to the lobby to go find out where Amere was.

After the front desk clerk gave me directions, I was on my way. As soon as I stepped out of the elevator and into the hallway that held Amere's room, I got butterflies. I walked slowly and looked inside each room until I got to his. I peeked in and noticed he was in his room alone. He laid in his bed as he watched TV, completely oblivious to the fact that I was watching him.

I cleared my throat to make my presence known and he still didn't look away from the TV. I took in his appearance and he still looks good, even with the wild facial hair and his desperate need of a haircut. "How you feeling?" I asked nervously, as I took a seat in the chair next to his bed. I sat there making small talk with my damn self because he wasn't responding to anything I was saying. "Listen, Tamia is here, so I have to go check on her. I'm going to write my number down and if you need anything, just call me," I said, as I scribbled my number down on a napkin.

"Tamia? She ok?" he asked and it pissed me off instantly. I had been sitting there a good ten to fifteen minutes and he hadn't responded to a thing I said. I mention Tamia on my way out the door and now, all of a sudden, he can talk.

"What's so damn special about Tamia?!" I snapped, as I walked up close to his bed. Surprise and shock filled his face as he looked at me with his eyes wide and mouth wider. "Oh, don't look at me like that! You never gave a fuck about her until she left you; now you're all up her ass! Everybody's all up her ass! See what ya'll do when I kill her ass!" I snapped and stormed out of the room.

Before I got to the elevator, I regretted every word that had rolled off of my tongue so effortlessly, but I knew it was too late to take it back. Now, in order for me to complete my mission, I have to kill Amere or get him to help me kill Tamia.

Amere

I've been laid up in this hospital bed since I got shot the fuck up and lost my daughter in the process. I don't care what those results said; I'm the only dad she has known in her life and no percentage on a sheet of paper could change that. I'm fucked up about her not being mine biologically though and for that, Lisa will pay. She caused me to lose the best thing that had ever happened to me over a lie. I lost a good girl that I know would have always had my back, had I treated her right when I had her.

When my mom first found out I was with Lisa, she told me karma was going to come back around and knock me on my ass for how I treated Tamia all of those years we were together. It turns out, karma didn't have to come back around because I ended up living with her. Lisa. Dealing with Lisa was great at first. She was a real freak and that's what I wanted. Tamia was a virgin when I met her so even though the pussy was good, she didn't know what to do to keep me satisfied. That damn Lisa had me the first time she did the monkey on this dick. She reeled me in with her sex game and took me off the line when she posted her sonogram online. When Tamia saw it, she was gone. I didn't even miss her right away. It wasn't until Lisa started showing her true colors that I started trying to get back with Tamia.

Lisa wasn't shit though and I hope karma is done with me because Lisa was a bit much to have to deal with. What I realize now that is really fucked up is how wrong I was for continuously hurting Tamia. I started fucking Armani and was splurging on the hoe like her and Tamia weren't best friends! I thought for sure that once Tamia found out about us that day that she would no longer deal with me or Armani.

I've been laying in this bed trying to figure out how I could right all of my wrongs and make things better for Tamia. I'm not even going to try to be with her because I know she deserves more than what I can give her. I had no idea how to make shit right until Armani came in my room on the bullshit. For one, I had no idea how she knew I was here or where to find me. Shit, on the coast, if you come to the hospital for a violent crime, you're made confidential, in case someone tries to come finish you off.

I never asked anyone about that at this hospital because I figured everybody involved in my shooting would think I was dead. Luckily for me, I survived but it's bad for them because I'll never forget the faces of everyone with a gun that dreadful day. The bitch that called it all together will get it the worse. I have dreamed about her every night and the things I'm going to do to her for killing my daughter.

First things first though, I need to start making things right with Tamia. The plan is to work on getting her to trust me and protect her from Armani. I want to just flat out tell her what she told me but she will think I've still been messing with her. I can't bring Armani's name up at all because I know it's going to remind her of the pain that I caused her.

I'm supposed to be released in a couple of days, so I need to get her number before she leaves or at least give her mines. I climbed out of bed slowly because of the pain. My body was still sore from the healing wounds and physical therapy that I have been going through.

I grabbed the walker from behind the door to brace myself, in case I got weak. The physical therapy is doing numbers but I still can't walk far without assistance. I used the walker to walk down to the elevator. Once I got on, I went down to the ground floor. When it reached the ground floor and the doors opened inside of the ER, I realized I had gotten on the employee elevator.

I made my way up and down two hallways, being careful to look in each room before I made it to Tamia's room. I stood in her doorway as I watched her and caught my breath from the long journey I had just gone on, just to see her. I wanted to say something but I didn't know what to say. Not only that but she looked like she was in deep thought.

She's still beautiful though, even with the fresh bruises on her face. All of the things she's gone through in her young life, you will never be able to tell by looking at her. I admire her strength and desire to be successful. She's going to go far and anyone that has come into contact with her is blessed. I stood there staring at her and regretting every tear that fell from her eyes because of me. All I want is one last chance to be a part of her life and all I want to do is be a friend. I finally built up enough courage to say something to her.

Tamia

I laid in the hospital bed trying desperately to figure out my next move. I'm learning now that I need to make sure I always have my own place. I went from having my own after my mom died to moving in and having to share a place with Armani. Then I moved out, so I wouldn't have to deal with her and moved in with Candy. Then I was going to move from her place to a place with Rashard. Now that all of those plans are damn near nonexistent, I have nowhere to go that I could call my own.

After talking to Jennifer again about cutting everybody off, she now has me rethinking my decision. I told her everything without leaving anything out. I went all the way back to my mom and her sickness. I told her about my relationship with Amere and why we broke up. I told her about Armani's abuse and what we did to Steve, which lead to us moving here. I spared no details about anything, not even what happened to Myra.

I told her I take full responsibility for Myra and Candy being laid up in the ER right along with me because I really believe it's my fault. I should have listened to Candy. Now I'm sitting in a hospital bed trying to understand everything. When it comes down to this coma business with Rashard, all I can think is how could he pretend to be in a coma? Then, I'm like how could Candy keep that from me? How could she help him deceive me?

Now I'm sitting here wondering why would he pretend to be in a coma and why would she help me? Hell, I'm sure he paid Doc; plus, Doc doesn't owe me shit but why would you put someone through that?

"I'm sorry," I heard a familiar voice say and it interrupted me from my thoughts. When I looked up, I had to do a double take at Amere as he stood in my doorway. I stared at him as he stood up and used a walker for support. He was in dire need of a haircut but still looked good. I could tell he was still a patient here in the hospital because he wore hospital scrubs and booties on his feet.

"Come in," I said and gestured for him to sit in the chair. This is the first time I've seen him and didn't get mad. I looked at him and sympathized mentally with his situation. Life is eating his ass up and I've never been one to kick someone while they're down.

"How you know I was here?" I asked, once he got situated in the chair. I watched the color drain from his face as he looked down and placed his hands on his knees. He took slow, deep breaths with his eyes closed and I had no idea what was wrong with him.

"I'm going to get help," I said and grabbed the call button, so I could call the nurse's station.

"No," he said, as he shook his head. "They will make me go back to my room," he explained and I sat the call button down. I didn't respond as I waited for him to regain control of whatever the hell he was trying to gain control of.

"I'm sorry about everything with Amiria," I said, as I looked at him. It took him a minute to nod his head and I felt like shit when he looked up. Amere had never been one to show emotions and I think that's why I thought we fit so well together because I don't either. The mentioning of a child passing the way Amiria past is enough to break anyone down though.

I could tell he was trying to hold back the tears but I could also see them threatening to fall. He has to let it out so he can mourn, so it will get easier to deal with. He placed his head inside the palms of his hands. I climbed out of bed slowly and fought through the pain. I stood next to Amere and wrapped my small arms around him.

"My baby gone," he belted out in a voice I didn't recognize. It was filled with pain and grief. The kind of pain that no parent ever wants to feel. He pressed his face into my stomach as he cried out for her. I continued to fight through the pain he was causing me as he wrapped his arms around my waist tightly and cried. "Not my baby, T," he sobbed uncontrollably as I rubbed his back. I didn't know what to say as I cried because he was hurting. I felt his pain but I knew he needed this.

I looked up at the door and saw Jennifer standing there with a worried expression on her face. When she recognized him and listened to him cry out for his baby girl, tears of her own cascaded down her brown cheeks. She walked away quickly, like she needed to get herself together. I stood next to him as silent as church mice, but I was in pain. My pain had to wait because someone needed me and even though all I'm able to do is stand here, I know it's enough.

About ten minutes later, his grip loosened and his arms dropped from around my waist. He lifted his head to look at me and his deep brown eyes drew me in. I know it was stupid but he needed this, and I just wanted to feel wanted. I wiped the tears from his face as we stared into each other's eyes. I bent over and kissed him on his full lips but softly at first. The kiss deepened and I felt him wrap his arms around me and pull me closer to him.

I could feel that all too familiar feeling between my legs. A feeling that has only been satisfied by the man before me. Images of all of the sex we use to have flashed through my mind as I moaned softly into his mouth. Almost instantaneously, the sonogram flashed through my mind, then the look on his face when I found about him and Armani. I pulled away and looked at him with sad eyes as a lump formed in my throat.

Rashard

I hauled ass back to the hospital after I talked to my Aunt Jennifer. She was about to let them wake Myra up now that my mom was there, so I need to be there when she opens her eyes. I know she's going to have to talk to the police too because they were outside of Candy's door trying to talk to her earlier today.

I can't believe Candy hadn't woken up yet and it's not because they have her heavily sedated, because they don't. Every time I asked my aunt about her, she would just say that it was touch and go and really all up to Candy when she woke up. When I talked to her on the phone and asked about Tamia, we got disconnected.

I pulled up into a parking spot and hopped out the car. I didn't realize I hadn't put it in park until it started rolling forward. I hopped back in the car quickly and threw the gear shaft in park and took the key out of the ignition. "Let's try this again," I said out loud to myself, as I power walked into the emergency room.

I could see Armani sitting in the waiting area but she was so engrossed in her phone that she didn't know I was back. "I'm trying to go back and see Myra Peterson," I said to the girl at the front desk. She rolled her eyes and picked the phone up.

"Can Peterson have another guest?" she asked whoever answered the phone. I frowned at her and tried to play nice, so I wouldn't have to shoot her or the big ass security guard she brought out here earlier. "Ok," she said and hung the phone up.

"Room 6, first-" I cut her off by walking away from her while she was trying to give me directions. I know where the fuck I'm going! Hell, the little bitch knows I was just here. I walked through the doors and headed to check on my baby sister. When I walked in her room, all eyes were on me. I glanced around the room and saw my mom, Ashley, and Aunt Jennifer. I'm sure they only let me back here because of Aunt Jennifer because they normally get on your damn nerves when they tell you only two can go back.

I walked up to my mom and waited for her to finish praying before I touched her back. When I heard the door close, I looked up to see that Aunt Jennifer closed it. "You let this happen to my baby over a bitch, Rashard?" my mom asked without raising her head.

It felt like all of the breath left my body when the reality of what she was saying hit me.

My mom was blaming me for this but I had nothing to do with it. I stood there seething with anger because I couldn't respond. I'll never disrespect my mom, so it's best that I just don't say anything at all. "It's not his fault," Aunt Jennifer said and my mom looked up at her.

"Didn't you say that nigga took my baby because he wanted the little bitch that my son has?!" my mom snapped at Aunt Jennifer.

My jaw hit the floor because I couldn't believe they knew what happened. "Mom, it's not his fault! It could have happened-"

"You right, it could have happened to any one of us! This could be you laying here or me! And where is she?" my mom snapped and cut Ashley off in the process.

"She's here too," I answered her somberly. I watched her shoulders relax like she was glad that Tamia got hurt too. "Candy too," I said because I felt it would be best to put it all out on the table now, instead of pissing her off with more bad news later.

She whipped her head around so she could face me so fast, I thought it was going to roll off her shoulders. "What the hell happened to Candy?" she asked, as she looked at me.

"He got her first," I said, as I shook my head.

"Oh my Lord! How is she?" she asked me, as she clenched her chest. I looked over at my aunt Jennifer for support.

"It's touch and go Janice. At this point, it's up to her," my Aunt Jennifer said.

"And where is he?" my mom asked me with a weird expression on her face.

"Dead," I answered her, as I looked directly into her eyes.

"Wait, you-"

"No, Tamia." I answered before she could ask me if I had killed him. Her eyes grew wide as the shock of what I said registered. A slow smile spread across her face.

"I like her," she said and my jaw hit the floor.

A few minutes ago, she was "that little bitch"; now she likes her. "I like her too," Aunt Jennifer said. "Shard, you know she's who I was going to try and hook you up with, right?" she asked and we laughed.

"I was already trying but she's hard to break down," I said and shook my head.

"That's because a woman isn't meant to be broken down son. Build her up and captivate her mind, then she's yours," my mom said to me. I looked around the room and both Ashley and Aunt Jennifer were nodding their heads.

Aunt Jennifer left because she had to get back to work. She told us to page her when Myra wakes up. "Where are all the kids?" I asked because it was getting late.

"With Bo," Ashley said and it shocked me. Normally, Bo only looks out for himself, so for him to take the time out and watch the kids for them is really admirable for him.

About ten minutes later, my mom's phone started ringing. "Hello... yes, this is she... a 911 call? Probably those kids, you can send a unit and scare their bad asses!... I'll be there shortly... yes, my son is there and will let you in... ok thanks, bye." I listened to my mom's one sided conversation. "Your bad ass kids called 911 again," my mom said to Ashley and we laughed.

"You not gone call and snap? You use to beat us!" I said, as I pretended to be jealous.

"Naw, you know Bo don't answer phones," she said and I nodded my head because she was right. You can call that man over and over, and he will not answer the phone.

"Well, let me go and check on my future wife. I'll be right back," I said and walked out of the door.

I walked to Tamia's room but she wasn't in there. *They must have moved her*, I thought to myself because I know Aunt Jennifer would have told me if she was discharged. I walked around the ER as I looked for her.

Once I found her room, I couldn't believe my eyes as I watched Tamia kiss someone else with so much passion. I wanted to believe that what I was seeing wasn't real. I wanted to believe that Tamia was different but I guess this is what I get for how I've treated women. To stand here and watch the woman I wanted to drop everybody for kiss another nigga like we wasn't planning to move in together fucked me up. I wanted to walk away but my feet didn't agree.

I was stuck. Planted in place. I couldn't move. I just watched. When she pulled away from the kiss, she didn't even look away from him. "I love you," he said, as he looked up at her.

"Amere," she said then closed her eyes and took a step back.

"This what we doing huh?" I asked calmly from the door. Amere turned his head and looked at me but didn't say a word. Tamia's hand subconsciously flew to her bottom lip, like she could take what she just did back.

She didn't say anything as she looked at me. I shook my head and walked away from the door. I can't believe this bitch played me and for the nigga that played her! This nigga cheated their whole relationship! This nigga fucked her best friend behind her back for years! This nigga ain't shit but this is the nigga she chose.

I shook my head and walked back to my sister's room. I wanted to go check on Candy but I didn't want to see "touch and go Candy". I wanted to see my sister that always has an attitude. I don't think I could handle seeing her the way she is now.

I could hear sobbing as I stood outside of Myra's room door. I barged in and mom was on the floor and Ashley was holding her. I looked at Myra and she looked fine. I could see her heart was still beating and everything.

"Mom, what's wrong?" I asked but she just continued to cry.

"The police just called and told her to get home now because something was wrong," Ashley said with tears in her eyes.

"What's wrong?" I asked because my thoughts went straight to the kids.

"They wouldn't say," Ashley said.

"Man, ya'll in here crying like the kids ain't there!" I snapped and stormed out the door.

"Where you going?" Ashley asked, as she ran behind me.

"Make sure my babies ok, ass!" I yelled at her. She hit the floor crying and yelling after my words hit her that the babies are home. I ran into Aunt Jennifer on my way out the door. "Can you go check on mama and Ashley? Something popped off at the house and I need to go check it out," I said as I bypassed her. I didn't wait for an answer because I need to make sure the kids straight.

Lisa

I laid on the floor pretending to be asleep through the whole ordeal. Call me what you want but I weighed my options when Bo first caught us in here and my best bet was to pretend to be knocked out! Hell, I know for a fact, Bo would have beat the shit out of me if I helped Michelle. I also knew that if I just stood and watched, Michelle would kill me. So yeah, I caught a quick nap on their ass! I listened to them duke it out until it got quiet.

I opened one of my eyes and saw he was about to rape her. I didn't want that to happen to no fucking body, so I started moving slowly. I was trying to talk myself into stabbing him in his back but the more logical me knew that this small ass knife I chose wouldn't do shit but piss him off, so I went back to sleep. Fuck it!

I was too happy when I heard the sirens because I knew Michelle was going to kill me. See, I think she saw me open my eyes but I can't be too sure, so I just pretended to stay sleep. I don't know how she was able to subdue him because I was too fucking scared to try and look again. Hell, it didn't even sound like rape to me. It sounded like they were fucking. "Damn, that's how she got em," I thought out loud to myself.

I waited until I heard the front door open and close before I opened my eyes. I sat up slowly because I was dizzy as fuck, so I knew I wasn't going to be able to get away. The sirens grew louder, so I knew they were closer. I crawled over to Bo and he was still alive but choking on his own blood. I grabbed his body and turned him on his side, so the blood would flow freely from his mouth.

"Stay... away... from... her," Bo said and coughed up more blood.

"Did ya'll have a baby?" I asked because I had heard everything they were saying to each other. He nodded his head and gripped my wrist tightly.

"She wanted… to trap… Ray. I got… her preg." He began coughing up more blood.

"Ssssshh. Stop trying to talk. Help is on the way," I said to him as I rubbed his head.

"She got… abortion," he said and soft cries distracted me.

I stood to my feet and ran out into the hallway. I saw three beautiful children standing in the hallway with the tallest one standing in the front. "Stay away from them!" the little girl said to me. It touched my heart that she wanted to stand up for the smaller kids. I was just glad that Michelle's psychotic ass had already left.

I went back into the room, so I could climb out of the window and run away. It took a minute but I was able to get it open. I looked out of the window and could see the officers running up to the front door. If I jump now, I can make a clean getaway.

"FREEZE!" I heard an officer yell once I got one leg out the window. I held my hands up high as another officer stormed in and rushed to Bo's aid. The officer that yelled at me approached me slowly, then snatched me out of the window roughly.

My leg started to sting and burn. I looked down at it and could see that my leg got cut on the window sill when he snatched me out of it. My pants leg was wet from blood. I reached down to pull my pants leg up to get a better look, but the officer kneed me in my back and pinned me down on the floor. "Ouch!" I yelled out.

"SHUTUP!" he yelled, as he patted me down.

I didn't have anything on me, not even my ID, because everything was in Michelle's car. The officer handcuffed me tightly and didn't remove his knee from my back the entire time we waited on the paramedics to come in and get Bo.

After they carried him out, the officer yanked me to my feet and I heard my shoulder pop. Tears sprang to my eyes instantly as my shoulder throbbed. I looked down at it and screamed at the top of lungs! It looked disfigured, so I knew he had dislocated my shoulder when he snatched me up off the ground. "SHUT…

UP!" he said through gritted teeth, as he shoved me towards the door. I cried harder with every step I took because my shoulder would not stop hurting.

When we made it on the porch, he shoved me again. I stumbled and fell down the stairs. The pain that ricocheted throughout my entire body was one I can't describe. I grinded my teeth together to keep from screaming out because it appears that my screams of agony are pissing him off. He grabbed my arm and yanked me off the ground.

I looked over at the kids who were huddled around the guy with dreads. I couldn't see his face because he was looking down at the kids as he talked to them. I know it's the infamous Rashard that's now with Tamia but use to be with Michelle. The same guy she tried to plant a baby on by getting his brother to get her pregnant. Pure unadulterated fuckery!

"What's your name?" the officer asked me as he waved Rashard over to me.

"Lisa. Lisa Cunningham," I answered him.

"Good evening son. I'm sorry to bother you but do you know this lady?" the officer asked Rashard, once he made it over to where we stood.

He examined my face as I examined his handsome face. Even though he was angry, he was still oh so sexy to me! "She fucked Rashard, so she had to go," replayed in my head in Michelle's voice and I looked away. If she will kill her own cousin for fucking with this man, I know she will kill me.

"Naw, I don't know her," he said to the officer but I could feel him staring at me.

When I looked up into his eyes, they had no emotion whatsoever, and it scared me far more than Michelle did. It scared me so much, I started answering questions that he hadn't even asked me. "I didn't do it!" I blurted out but his eyes got darker.

"Shut up!" the officer yelled in my face. Spit flew from his mouth but I was too caught up in Rashard to look away from him or even acknowledge anyone else at this moment.

He glanced around and then slid his thumb across his throat slowly. Everybody knows what that means; hell, even green people that have never even been to the hood. "Nooo! I didn't do it! You gotta believe me! Please believe me!" I begged because I didn't want to die.

The officer opened the police car door and pushed me inside. I screamed out in pain because I landed on my shoulder. I shook it off quickly, so I could look at Rashard. He was still standing in the same spot with the same look in his eyes. "It was Michelle!" I screamed out to him as a final attempt to stop him from killing me. I thought I saw something in his facial expression change but I couldn't be sure.

The kids ran up to him and the look vanished as he got down on his knees and talked to them. "Why'd you stab that boy?" an officer asked after he sat in the driver's seat. He pulled off and when I looked back at Rashard, he was smiling at me. That smile was far worse than the look he was just giving me. A chill went down my spine.

I rather go to jail than be on the run from him and Michelle, I thought to myself.

Armani

As I sat in the lobby, I began to panic about the things I said to Amere out of anger. I have no idea how to fix it other than going back up to talk to him. When I made it to his room, I had everything that I wanted to say already at the tip of my tongue, but his room was empty. I tried to ask a nurse on the floor where he went but nobody knew.

That's how I ended up back out here in the lobby. I didn't know what to do to fix this mess. For some reason, the quote Tamia had on the wall in her room was stuck in my head. It was huge and in black and white. It said "We can't solve problems by using the same kind of thinking we used when we created them." I can't tell you who said it because I don't remember. I don't even know why I remember the freaking quote because he doesn't make any sense! How the fuck can I use different thinking when this is the only way I know how to think?

"Fuck!" I said out loud because now I have to go home to Joe. I stood up to walk out of the ER but I saw Rashard heading inside, so I sat back down. I started to scroll through my Facebook news feed as I waited for him to finish whatever he was about to do. I sat there with my fingers crossed that they let him back and nearly jumped for joy when they let him in the back. I needed to know where he was, in case Joe needed to know when I made it home.

I quickly stood to my feet and headed out to my car. I stopped at the gas station to get some Tylenol for the pain I was about to receive. Then, it hit me; this is the first time that I didn't lose him and I have news other than who he's fucking! I felt pumped as I turned the radio on and plugged my phone into the auxiliary chord, so I could listen to my music. Of course, I had to play my girls Nicki Minaj and Beyoncé because I was indeed feeling myself.

I rapped along to the lyrics at the stop light. I was going all in like I was Nicki Minaj in concert. I was so excited and amped up that I threw my truck in park at the light and changed the song to Throw some mo by Nicki Minaj and Rae Sremmurd.

I climbed on the hood of my truck with the music blasting as the beat dropped. The light turned green and the people behind me started to blow their horns but I didn't care because I was in the zone.

Ass fat, yeah I know
You just got cash? Blow some mo'
Blow sum mo', blow sum mo'
The more you spend it, the faster it go
Bad bitches, on the floor
It's rainin' hundreds, throw sum mo'
Throw sum mo' throw sum mo'
Throw sum mo', throw sum mo'

I was on top of my hood throwing it in a circle to the beat as Nicki Minaj sang her hook. I was bouncing it all over the place until this guy pulled over and offered me a job. I thought it was so funny that I actually got in my car and followed him. When we were talking, he made it sound like he had this hot club that was jumping but I followed him to this little hole in the wall juke box looking joint.

I climbed out of my truck with a look of disgust on my face. "Never judge a book by its cover," Raphael said to me. I looked at him and smiled, then followed him inside the club. As soon as we walked through the doors of Carte Blanche, I was in awe. The place looks amazing! I've never thought I would work at a club. Hell, I never thought I would work period, yet here I am.

"Damn," I said out loud when I looked up and saw bitches in cages. There were four cages total, one in each corner.

"Follow me," he said and lead the way to his office. "Do you work?" he asked and I shook my head no. I don't have any experience doing shit but fucking. I need to get to a computer, so I can get my sponsors' phone numbers out of my google drive files. I need to contact them, so I can make amends and hopefully get back in their good graces. "I like the show you put on in the road. You ever dance before?" he asked and I shook my head no. I couldn't believe someone was offering me a job.

"One of my cage girls decided she doesn't want to partake in cage dancing anymore. Would you like that position?" he asked me and I frowned my face up.

"How long will I have to stay in there?" I asked because I needed to make sure I covered all bases.

"Your entire shift, six hours," he answered, like six hours wasn't shit.

"Oh, uh un nigga! What if I have to piss or get hungry?" I asked him, seriously hoping we will get a lunch break like normal people.

"Do all of that after your shift," he said, as he sat back and interlaced his fingers across his stomach.

I grabbed my purse and stood up to leave. "That's cruel Raphael. I'm not dancing for six hours straight with no type of break," I said after I stopped at the door.

"It pays $5,000 a night," he said and it stopped me in my tracks.

"$5,000?" I asked, just to be sure I heard him correct. Shit, if I could make that much a night alone, I won't need my sponsors! Then maybe I could fix shit with Amere and be with him.

"Ok, I'll take it. When can I start?" I asked.

"Now. C'mon, let me show you where you will be able to shower and change clothes," he said, as he ushered me out of the office. We walked into the dressing room and all eyes landed on me.

"I'm Armani," I said to the ladies that were in the dressing room but nobody responded.

"What she gone be doing?" some really, really black chick asked Raphael.

He looked at me as if he was waiting on me to answer her, but what I was thinking, I'm sure he did not want me to say. "She's the new cage dancer," he answered.

"Wait, she's taking Candy's spot?! I asked you for that!" she yelled, as she stood to her feet. I didn't care about her attitude; all I wanted to know is if she's talking about the same chick that stole my best friend! I know I can't just come out and ask them about Candy because they don't know me. I'm sure if she still works here, we will run into each other though.

"Baby, you must can't do this?" I asked, as I turned around and made my ass clap. I bent over slightly and threw it in a circle slowly at first, then I sped up. I dropped low and made it bounce and popped back up. When I turned back around, two bad bitches were clapping for me. I winked at them and focused my attention back on the monkey in front of me.

She sucked her teeth and rolled her eyes at Raphael. He chuckled lightly then turned to face me. "Good job," he said. "Tia, Megan, help her get situated and teach her the ropes. Her shift starts in two hours," he said and walked out of the dressing room.

A dark skinned thick chick with a bob stood up and waved me over. "I'm Tia and this is Megan," she said, as she pointed to the brown skin chick that was sitting on ass for days. She looked up at me and smiled before she focused back on what she was doing. I looked over her shoulder and saw that she was doing her own fingernails.

"Oooh girl, you da truth!" I exclaimed because she was doing the damn thing.

I took the empty seat next to her and sat there as I waited for them to tell me what to do. "You're more my size, so I'll give you one of my outfits that I've never worn and when you get paid tonight, just give me $40," Tia said and I nodded my head. I could feel someone staring a hole in the back of my head and when I turned around, it was that real dark chick.

"What's the deal with that chick?" I turned back around and asked.

"Who, Goldie?" Tia asked and I gave her a confused look. I looked back and didn't see anyone that looks like they would be called Goldie.

"No girl! That extraterrestrial black ass bitch that got an attitude a few minutes ago," I said and pointed at the girl. Megan started laughing so hard tears were falling from her eyes.

"Yo, that's the same shit ole girl said that hosted Deuce's party!" Megan said to Tia.

"Damn sholl was when she snapped out on her. What was her name?" Tia asked.

"Tamia. She came through and switched everything up and gave everybody new jobs and shit," Megan said to me.

"Yea but everybody made money that night though, so she knew what she was doing," another girl chimed in.

I turned around to look and it was a brown skinned chick talking. She was cute but she ain't have a lick of ass! "Ashley," she said with her hand extended.

"Armani," I said and shook her hand. I glanced over at Goldie and knew I was about to make her life a living hell. I noted that they all know Tamia but I have to make sure they're feeling her before I decide where this friendship goes.

Michelle

I can't believe we just killed Bo in his mom's house! That was so careless because she lives in a good neighborhood. Someone probably saw us climbing through the window and called the police. I'm just glad I got out of there before the police got there. Too bad for Lisa because she's going to take the fall for it. Hopefully, she's not too mad at me for leaving her unconscious to take a murder charge but it ain't like she got kids or anything to stay out of jail for.

I'll finish off our mission since she's going to jail. If she's smart and never been in trouble, she will go incognito so they won't know her real identity. "Fuck, I shouldn't have left her there," I said out loud to myself as I continued to drive.

I drove all the way home without stopping, so I could hop in the shower and change clothes. I washed the gel out of my hair so it would be wet and wavy, then headed back out the door. I stopped at Wendy's and ordered a Jr bacon cheeseburger and some fries. Once I was done eating, I hopped back on the road.

I rode in silence, so I could figure out my next move. I checked the back seat to make sure my bag was still there, so I didn't have to stop and get a knife and it was. About fifteen minutes later, I pulled up to Dre's apartment complex. I checked the parking lot to make sure no one was watching me. It's dark so they wouldn't be able to give a good description anyway.

"What's up?" Twan asked, as I passed by him on the staircase.

"Too much of nothing," I answered as I kept it moving. I was on a mission and I didn't have time to have idle chit chat with someone who doesn't even fucking like me.

"Where's Lisa?" he asked and it pissed me off.

"Lisa's minding her own damn business! Maybe you should too!" I snapped at him and he took a step towards me.

He walked all the way up to me on the staircase. We were so close that I could feel his breath on my face. "Bitch, don't you ever disrespect me again!" he said through clenched teeth. I smiled as I looked him directly into his eyes. We stared at each other for about ten seconds, then I licked the tip of his nose.

He frowned his face up at me and I felt him press his gun against my side. I looked down at the gun and back up into his eyes. "You wanna shoot me?" I asked, and I could see he was clenching his jaws.

"Don't ever disrespect me again," he said, as he removed the gun from my side.

"Never pull a gun out and not use it," I said, then pushed him as hard as I could. He flew in the air and missed the rest of the steps. He landed on his back with a hard thud. I could hear him grunting as he looked up at me with wide eyes. A small puddle of blood began to form under his head. I winked at him and turned to go have a talk with Dre.

I knocked on the door softly at first but he didn't answer it. I started knocking a bit harder and one of his neighbors swung their door open. "He must not be home!" she snapped with a frown on her face.

"Bitch, mind ya fuckin business!" I snapped back at her. She rolled her eyes and slammed her door.

Right when I was about to knock again, Dre opened his door and snatched me inside of his apartment. "What?!" he yelled, like I had done something to piss him off.

"What's ya problem?" I asked with my hand on my hip.

"You out here beatin on my fuckin door like you da police!" he snapped, still visibly upset.

I dropped down to my knees and pulled the drawstring on his sweatpants because I know that sex is the easiest way to kill men. I need him vulnerable, so he won't put up much of a fight. I need to be able to distract him enough to do what needs to be done. I have to go ahead and kill him, so Lisa won't become a snitch. I know I shouldn't have left her but I wasn't exactly myself at the time.

"What you doing?" he asked, as he looked behind me. I was confused until I thought about it.

"I've been thinking about you. We gotta make it quick. I drugged her, so I could come please you," I said. The way that lie rolled off my tongue with ease shocked me but he bought it. His dick was hard from the moment I snatched his pants down, so I took the head into my mouth slowly.

It wasn't until I started trying to take him deeper that I remembered I'd never been all that good at sucking dick. Ray use to love it until he got head from somebody that sucked it better than I did. I looked up at Dre and he had his eyes closed as he moaned softly. He tried to force more of his dick in my mouth but I started to gag. I pulled back and swallowed to ease my sensitive gag reflexes.

"What the fuck?" he asked, as he slapped me across my face with his dick. It hit me in the eye and caused it to burn. I tried to rub my eye but he grabbed my short hair and guided my mouth back to his dick. I grabbed the shaft with my hand and began to stroke it as I sucked the head. His grip tightened as he bobbed my head faster and faster. He snatched my hand away from his dick and slapped me so hard that I lost my balance and fell on the floor.

Missy

"This bitch can't do shit right!" I thought to myself, as I sat on the floor. I could taste the blood in my mouth, which let me know that my lip was busted. I looked up at Dre as anger took over my body. "You shouldn't have done that," I said calmly. He looked at me with a frown on his face as he tilted his head to the side. He walked over to me slowly with a menacing look on his face. I looked up at him and noticed the white residue under his nose for the first time.

Bitch didn't tell me he was a coke head, I thought to myself as I stood to my feet. "The fuck you just say to me?" Dre asked, as he grabbed my neck and pushed me into the wall. He had a tight grip on me but I wasn't about to allow him to take me down as easily as Bo had. I glanced down and noticed his dick was still hanging.

I stretched my arm out and grabbed his dick and gripped it as tight as I could. He made an animalistic noise as he dropped down to his knees, which brought me down in the process. "Let... me... go!" he said between forced breaths. I squeezed harder and he released my neck and tried to pry my hand off of his dick. I used my other hand and grabbed his balls and squeezed just as hard. He roared and threw both hands in the air above his head. I looked up just in time to see him bringing both fists down at the same time to hit me.

I quickly let go and tumbled out of the way. He punched the floor over and over with his free hand because his other hand flew to his dick when I let it go. He whimpered softly as he rocked back and forth holding his dick and balls. "I always say all a man has in this world is his word and his balls, and I just damn near took one of the two," I said with a laugh.

He looked at me with a look of death and if looks alone could kill, I know I'd be a dead woman. Too bad for Dre that I tumbled right to my back pack. I quickly dug through the back and grabbed two knives because I was ready to do some serious damage.

I stood to my feet and approached him slowly as he looked at me without moving a single muscle. As soon as I was close enough to swing, I did but I wasn't fast enough. Dre swung hard and the blow caught me in the stomach. That Jr bacon cheeseburger and fries wasted no time erupting from the pits of my stomach. It landed all over Dre's face and clothes.

He jumped up to his feet as he looked down at the vomit as it slid all over him. I quickly reached out and stabbed him in his stomach while his focus was no longer on me. I yanked the knife right back out and watched the blood pour from his wound. I used the knife that was in my other hand to stab him in his back before he had time to attack me again. My stomach hurt like hell but I ignored the pain as I stabbed him in his stomach and back again at the same time. I snatched the knife back out of his stomach and he fell forward. My grip on the knife that was still lodged in his back caused me to fall with him.

I quickly stood back up and pulled with all of my might, but I couldn't get the knife out. I stepped down on his back, so I could pull at a better angle and when it finally came out, I fell backwards, hit the TV, and then the floor. I closed my eyes as I caught my breath and when I opened them, the TV and its stand were falling over. I tried to roll out of the way but I didn't move in time. The TV landed hard on my back and my head hit the floor.

I laid on the floor and watched the blood drain from the gash that formed when my head hit the floor. I tried to get up but I was too weak to move. I know I needed to go before Dre got up but I had none of the energy I would need to move the TV.

I began to try to slide from under the TV once I heard Dre grunting. I didn't want him to get up and kill me before I had the chance to kill him. The more I scooted over, the more discouraged I got because the TV was still on my back. After a few minutes of trying, I gave up and just laid on the floor trapped underneath the TV.

Tamia

I stood completely still with my mouth wide open as I stared out into the hallway at the spot Rashard was just standing in. The look on his face was one of pure hurt and disappointment. I know I was debating about whether or not I should cut him off, but I still didn't want to hurt him in the process. I wanted to run after him, so I could apologize for what he saw. If I could take it back, I would, but I can't.

"Don't worry T. He just needs time," Amere said, as he reached out to touch my hand. I took a step away from him and sat back down on the bed.

"Naw, I'm pretty sure it's over with," I said, as I laid back against the pillow on the bed. I didn't know what to do to fix this. Hell, I didn't even know if I wanted to fix it. I stared up at the ceiling, trying to figure out what I was going to do. I'm not the type of female to chase any nigga because I know there's more to life than that and the world won't end because we aren't going to date anymore. Now, at the same time, I don't want any bad blood with anyone.

It took years for me to forgive Amere for the pain he's caused me and I didn't even realize I had forgiven him until he showed up tonight. When I saw him and didn't feel any ill feelings towards him, I knew that I was over it. I only kissed him because it's been months since I felt wanted and even longer since I've been touched. I wasn't thinking clearly because the sex that I knew would have been explosive was on my mind.

"You're a good woman. You made a mistake and I'm sure he has too. He'll get over it," Amere said and it shocked me. I halfway expected him to be trying to push up on me but here he is, just being a friend. It's strange as hell talking to him about another man, but it's great not to be alone.

"I'm not sure I want him to get over it. I care if it hurt him but not enough to chase em, ya know?" I asked because I don't know if the way I feel makes sense when I say it out loud.

"T, I'm about to tell you some real shit and don't get offended. You selfish as fuck when it comes to dating," he said, as he looked at me from the chair that he was sitting in.

"How?" I asked with a frown because I don't think I'm selfish at all.

"All you think about is yourself and when you're in a relationship, it's not just you no more," he said and it sounded like the biggest load of shit I had ever heard in my entire life! People say "It's not just you" when you have children and I don't have any, so why should I say that about a nigga? "Naw, I disagree," I said, as I shook my head at him.

"With you being selfish or what I just said?" he asked, as he watched me intensely.

"Both! I'm not selfish Amere; I'll help anybody that needs me," I said defensively. He didn't respond; he just shook his head.

I watched him walk over to the counter and grab my cellphone, then he tossed it to me. "Unlock it and put my number in it, so we can text," he said and I gave him the side eye. "Girl chill, don't nobody want your big headed ass," he said and I laughed. That was the first time I had a real genuine laugh in a while. I unlocked the phone and saved his number and he left.

A few minutes later, Jennifer came in and checked my vitals. "You look tired Tamia," she said and I believe her because I was. I don't know what time it was but I knew it was getting late.

"I am but I don't think I'm going to be able to fall asleep," I said to her as I shook my head.

"Ole lord, what done happened now?" she asked, as she took a seat in the chair Amere was just sitting in. I gave her a run through of what happened and what Rashard saw. She shook her head and stared at the floor for a few minutes before she answered. "Let me tell you something about Rashard," she said, as she stood to her feet and closed the door.

I watched her walk back to the chair and sit down before she continued. "That boy been a hoe for as long as I can remember, even when he had a girlfriend. I'll bet you any kind of money that since ya'll being doing whatever the hell ya'll lil confused asses been doing that he's still been doing him," she said and paused, like she was letting it sink in. I nodded my head in agreement because I do feel like he's been hiding something from me.

I stared at her as I waited for her to continue. "Even if ya'll not together though, apologize for what he saw because you have to put yourself in his shoes. Yea, you were thinking about cutting him but he didn't know anything about that. He thought ya'll were about to be together and move in together, and he walked in on you kissing your ex," she said then shrugged her shoulders.

"I have to go get my computer, so I can administer some meds and I'll be back to give you yours," she said and left as quickly as she had come. I laid there in deep thought because what she said made sense. I grabbed my phone and quickly shot him a text.

Tamia: im sorry for what you walked in on. it shouldn have happened. im sorry i did it too.

I didn't know what else to say to him other than that. I sat there with the phone in my hand for thirty minutes waiting on a reply that I never got. I shook my head as I looked up just as Jennifer was walking back into the room. She scanned my armband, then administered my shot intravenously. She gave me a cup with two pills in it. "This is for swelling," she said, as she gestured towards the cup. I took the pills and laid back down.

"How is Myra?" I asked before she turned to walk away.

"She's fine. In pain but she's alive. She was awake but I think she's sleeping right now," she answered me. I smiled and nodded my head.

"Um... Jennifer!" I called out when she reached the door.

"Yes?" she answered.

"Never mind. Thanks," I said as I shook my head.

"She's fine. She woke up about an hour ago asking for you," Jennifer said and walked out of the door. I nodded my head, even though she couldn't see me. My eyelids grew heavier and heavier as sleep overcame.

Rashard

I waited until the police officer pulled off to make the call that I'd been wanting to make since I found out what happened. "What's up boss?" he said and I laughed. Thoughts of Candy filled my mind but I quickly shook them away.

"Aye, squad car 7586 has someone I need in it. Just left mom dukes house," I said directly into the receiver. I looked around the yard and knew nobody was paying me any attention, except for my nieces and nephew.

"Gotcha covered boss. We already on this end," Tre said.

"Why?" I asked, simply out of curiosity.

"Just dropped Deuce off to Candy," he answered.

"Oh ok! That's what's up," I said, as I nodded my head. I disconnected the call and sat down on the side of the road to talk to my nieces and nephew.

"Hey ya'll wanna go see ya'll mama?" I asked and they all nodded their heads. I could tell they were tired and I was about to pull an all-nighter because I needed to figure out what the fuck was going on. The ambulance had already pulled off with Bo in the back of it, so I guess everyone will be staying the night in the damn emergency room. Maybe Ashley will get the kids and take them home with her though because I got moves to make.

When we made it to the hospital and walked in the ER, there was a different girl at the front desk. I shook my head because I didn't have time for no bullshit. "Hey, excuse me. I'm Rashard and my sister Myra Peterson is in the back. I need to drop these kids off to my other sister," I explained to her. She looked up with a big smile on her face and just hit the button, so the doors would open for me. "Thanks ma," I said and headed to the back with the kids.

I walked in the room without knocking and everybody was asleep. Aunt Jennifer had already texted me and told me she was awake, but I was handling shit. My phone vibrated in my hand

and when I opened it, I shook my head at Tamia's bullshit ass apology. She can keep that shit because she showed me why I don't trust these bitches.

"Ashley, wake up," I said, as I shook her lightly. I needed her awake before I told my mom what happened to Bo.

"What?" she answered groggily.

"Man, get up," I said, as I shook her harder and she stood up. When I turned to face my mama, she was already awake and looking at me.

"What happened?" she asked and it caught me off guard. I wasn't expecting her to be so alert and ready.

"Somebody broke in the house and stabbed Bo. He's here but I don't know where. I was bringing Ashley the kids, so I could get things handled," I said to her in one breath and she nodded her head.

"Take them babies to yo house, so they can lay down," my mama said to Ashley. She nodded her head and walked out of the room.

"I'll be back tomorrow," I said, as I walked to the door.

"Be careful son. Kill them but be careful," my mama said to me and my jaw hit the floor. "Oh, so you been thinking mama was a fool all these years, huh? You ain't had no wool over my eyes baby! The only reason you hadn't heard my mouth is because you kept school first and nothing ever happened to us. This girl got you sloppy," she said, as she looked at me with a concerned expression on her face.

The mention of Tamia pissed me off and I'm sure by the way my mom started looking at me that my facial expression showed it. "What she do already, hell?" my mom asked. "You know what? Fuck her. Go get your head in the game baby; I love you," she said with a dismissive wave of her hand.

I walked out of the hospital just as my phone started ringing. "Yea?" I answered the phone.

"Packaged intercepted, we in the dungeon," and then the call disconnected. I hopped in my car and headed to the dungeon for the second time today.

When I pulled up, I saw the flash of a red beam go across my eye. I stopped the car and stepped out of it, so Peanut could see it was me from wherever he was before he killed me. "Sorry!" I heard him yell off in the distance.

"Can't be too careful," I yelled back, even though I didn't know where he was. I hopped back in my car and drove down to the same parking spot I was parked in earlier.

Tre opened the door to a different house than he was in, so I walked over to him. "What's up; this ain't Chardae in here bruh," Tre said confused, as he dapped me up.

"That bitch damn near killed my brother tonight. Police got to her before I did," I explained, as I locked the door and followed him down to the basement.

"This bitch been crying and begging since I grabbed her. I had to dead the police officer and take the camera out his car," Tre said, as he walked right up to the chick and slapped her already battered face.

"What the hell you do to her shoulder, nigga?" I asked because it looked like a football injury.

"Naw fam, that shit was like that when I grabbed her," he said, as he shook his. I didn't know they rough bitches up like that too. I guess they really don't care.

I walked up to her, pulled out my pocket knife, and cut her free. "What you doing?" Tre asked. I pulled her arm and popped her shoulder back in place, then tied her back up.

"What's your name?" I asked, to make sure I heard her correctly when she told the police.

"Lisa. I didn't do that to your brother; it was Michelle," she said and caught me by surprise at how easy it was to get her talking.

"Michelle?" I asked to make sure she was talking about the same one I'm thinking about. She didn't respond right away and Tre punched her in the face again. She spit blood out of her mouth and began to beg us to let her go. I shook my head at her, so she knew she wasn't going anywhere.

"Ok, it's the Michelle you use to date. I'll tell you everything if you let me go," she said, trying to bargain.

"Bitch, you gone tell me everything anyway," I said with a smile on my face. The fact that she thought she had the upper hand in this situation was quite comical.

"Tell me what you know about Michelle or it's gonna get worse than a punch," I said and her eyes grew big and filled with alarm.

"Michelle wants to kill Tamia," she blurted out and it caught me by surprise. I didn't let it show as I nodded my head because I already know why she wants to kill her.

"What else?" I asked. My facial expression showed her that I wasn't the least bit impressed.

"The baby she was pregnant with was your brother baby. She… she… she got an abortion because you didn't believe her," she rambled out and I couldn't hide the shock. I looked over at Tre and I could tell her revelation caught him by surprise as well.

"Wow," Tre said, as he looked between us. I bet this was like a Jerry Springer episode to this nigga.

"Is that why she wanted him dead? Was he gonna tell me or something?" I asked, as I tried to understand why she would go to this extreme. Michelle was never the violent type when we were together, so I wonder what made her snap.

"He beat her til she passed out. She told him she would kill him and let him go so she had to go back and kill him first," she answered me, as she looked around nervously.

"Is that all?" I asked and she nodded her head.

I pulled my pistol out and cocked it back. "Wait, it's a lot of people gunning for you," she rushed out.

"Tell me something I don't know," I said and she didn't respond.

"I should have stayed with Dre," she said, right before two bullets to the dome silenced her for life.

"Man, why you kill her?" Tre asked.

"Reflex, we'll figure out who else is involved when we find Michelle. Dre is easy to find," I said, as we walked back up the steps and left.

Armani

My first night at the club was amazing! Tiresome but still amazing! My feet hurt like hell from dancing in 6" stilettos all night and my back ached, but it's nothing a nice hot bath couldn't fix. Hell, those hot baths got me through plenty of ass whoopings delivered by Joe. The thought of him made me not want to go home but I have nowhere else to go.

Megan and Tia are going to have drinks but I'm tired and sore, so I just want to go home and relax. Hopefully, Joe is satisfied with the information I have and not concerned with the time I'm going to make it in. I checked my phone and realized he hasn't texted me or called me all day long, so he must have had a really busy day.

I hopped in my truck and drove home with tunnel vision. At this moment, all I care about is the tub that I'm about to fill with hot water and bath beads. When I made it to the condos, I climbed out and head inside of the building.

"Long day?" James, the security guard asked.

"Yes, my body is aching!" I exclaimed, as I made my way to the elevator. "Is he home?" I turned around and asked, but he shrugged his shoulder.

"I haven't seen him," he said, then focused his attention on the monitors in front of him. At the same time, the elevator chimed and the doors opened. I climbed in as I stared down at my phone, willing it not to ring before I got in the condo. If he doesn't call, then maybe I'll have peace while I relax.

"We're not speaking?" a familiar voice asked. When I looked up and came face to face with him, I didn't know how to feel. I wanted to be mad because I reached out for help when I was being kidnapped, and he left me hanging. I wanted to be mad because he wanted to date me, and Tamia never mentioned it to me. Then, on the other hand, I've been wanting to see him because I miss the dick and I'm not used to working. I didn't think I could make it without my sponsors but this $5,000 that I made tonight proves otherwise.

"Hey Daddy," I said sheepishly.

"I been needing you. I knew you were free but it took me a minute to figure out where you were," he said and I felt my body stiffen at the mention of me being free. Yes, I'm no longer being held captive but I'm still a prisoner. I'm being forced to follow someone daily and anytime that I lose him, I get beat. I can fight and I'd probably win, but I wouldn't have anywhere to go after that. So, um yeah, I'm not free, so I didn't respond.

When the elevator opened at my floor, I looked back to tell Dave bye but he grabbed my arm and snatched me close to him. I could feel him breathing heavily on the top of my head. "Why you smell like smoke?" he asked, as he took a step away from me. The doors of the elevator closed and I sighed heavily.

"I was at the club," I answered, as I hit the button to go back down to my floor. The elevator had already taken off so I would have to wait until Dave got off, so I could head back home and hopefully, make it there before Joe.

"You club now?" he asked, as he looked at me as if he was trying to see into my soul. I shrugged my shoulders in response and stepped backwards, so I could lean against the wall. When the doors opened again, Dave stepped off. "C'mon," he said, as he looked at me. Fear took over my body and I began to tremble at the thought of someone else touching me. If Joe came home and wanted to fuck and thought I gave this pussy to someone else, he would body me for sure. "What's wrong with you?" Dave asked and I shook my head to let him know I was fine.

"That's ya boyfriend now, huh?" Dave asked with a hurt look on his face. I shook my head again as I continued to look down at my feet. I could feel Dave's body heat as he stood in front of me. His Gucci Guilty cologne invaded my nose as I closed my eyes and inhaled deeply. My pussy began to tingle as my clit throbbed while thoughts of the sex we'd had filled my mind. "Let's go," he said and grabbed my hand.

I followed him into the penthouse that he has other than the home he shares with his wife, Sabrina. I stood dormant as I took in the surroundings. Everything was still the same as the last time I was here. He walked off in the direction of the bathroom and I heard the shower come on. "Mani, c'mere!" he yelled and I quickly headed in his direction.

I stood in the doorway and admired his naked toned body from behind as he bent over the tub. "Get naked," he said and I quickly stripped down to nothing. He turned and held his hand out for me to grab. He helped me climb in the tub slowly and thoughts of the hot bath I wanted to soak in clouded my mind. The water pressure from the shower head felt amazing as it pummeled my skin. I stood directly under the spray of water with my eyes closed. I felt Dave's presence behind me as he began to wash my body. Once he was done with my back, he turned me around so he could wash the front, then handed me the towel to finish.

He grabbed my shoulders and pushed me softly directly under the stream of water. I could feel my hair sticking to my skin as he tilted my head back. I kept my eyes closed as he started massaging my scalp. I could smell the cherry scent coming from the shampoo and he continued to massage my scalp.

He kissed me softly on my neck, then in random places all over my body. It took me a minute to realize he was kissing bruises. Tears began to stream down my face but the water hid them well. After all of the shampoo rinsed out of my hair, I kissed him hungrily. We kissed with so much passion that I didn't know what to do next. This was a time that I wasn't in control and the plan was to let him lead.

He broke the kiss and made his way down to my breasts. He grabbed and nibbled on my nipple as his free hand found its way to my pussy. He inserted two fingers and moved them around until he found my spot. He stroked it over and over as I moaned out on a verge of cumming, then he stopped.

I released a frustrated sigh as I opened my eyes and looked into his. We stared at each other so deep with so much love and I couldn't understand it. Never in my life had I ever felt like this before. He cupped my face in his hands and kissed my lips softly as the water sprayed us both. He slid his hands down my body until he reached my legs. He grabbed one and propped it on the side of the tub.

I watched him get down on his knees and suck on my clit with so much force, I almost came right then. He inserted two fingers as he sucked vigorously. I threw my head back in pure ecstasy as he devoured my pussy. It didn't take long for my legs to start trembling. I thought I was going to fall but he cupped my ass and pulled me closer, like the juices that were pouring from my body weren't enough. I moaned out as he continued to lap at my pussy like his very survival depended on this very moment. My legs grew weaker as I came again. He gripped me tighter but it wasn't enough to stop me from hitting the floor of the bathtub.

My knees buckled and feet slipped but he grabbed my arms before my head hit the back of the tub. The bathroom filled with laughter once everything registered. I just bust my ass while getting my pussy ate in the shower! Don't try that shit at home! Well, at least not without one of those tub mats that prevents shit like this.

"You good?" Dave asked, once we caught our breath from laughing. I looked at his handsome face that was still wet but I couldn't tell if it was the water or my sweet juices.

"Yes," I answered and looked away. I didn't look away because I was embarrassed, it was because I was seeing a side of Dave I had never seen. Our relationship had been strictly platonic with no emotions involved; now he's showing a softer side.

He reached over my head and turned the water off, stood to his feet, and helped me to mine. He carried me from the bathroom to his room and made love to me for the first time, and I loved every minute of it.

For the first time in my life, I went to sleep at peace with nothing but happy thoughts as Dave snuggled closely behind me.

Tamia

6 weeks later...

Believe it or not, it took Rashard three days before he talked to me again and I was more than excited to hear his ring tone, even though it was just a text message. I was hospitalized for four days and as dumb as it may sound, I crashed at Amere's place. I was released a day before him and we had talked so much that he knew about me wanting to cut everyone off possibly, and he gave me a key to his place.

At first, I was bit skeptical but he hasn't hit on me at all, not even once. Hell, a few nights I wanted some so bad that I walked out of my room wearing only a tank top shirt and thongs, and he still didn't try so I gave up because I knew he's not what I need. I start work tomorrow, so hopefully I can move out in a couple of weeks and get my own place. It was getting harder and harder to keep where I live away from Rashard. I completely stopped leaving out of the house because I thought he would see me and follow me back to Amere's place.

Candy is much better and Deuce hasn't left her side. Myra got released a day before I did and she doesn't blame me for what happened to her, which is totally awesome because I had been blaming myself.

"What you cookin ma?" Amere asked, as he stood in the kitchen.

"Bacon, egg, and cheese sandwiches," I answered, as I scooped the eggs out of the skillet and into a bowl, so they wouldn't stick or burn. He looked a bit nervous as I busied myself with fixing our sandwiches.

"What's wrong?" I asked and he looked away.

"You been a great friend to me, so let me be one to you," I pressed. He sighed deeply then focused his deep brown eyes on me.

"I haven't talked to Lisa at all. All of her things are gone but she's not answering her phone," he said, as he waited for me to respond to him.

"You should file a missing person's report. Has she ever done this before?" I asked.

"Naw, but all of this shit with Amiria, ain't no telling what's goin on in her mind," he said, as he shook his head. I nodded mine in agreement as my phone dinged, indicating I had a text message. I watched Amere to see if he was going to continue before I checked the message.

Rashard: ready 2 cme hme?

Tamia: home?

Rashard: da house I bought u

Tamia: only if u won't b there

Rashard: i jux want u safe

Tamia: k

Rashard: wats da address we can move ur stuff now

Tamia: i got it covered

I looked up at Amere and didn't know how to tell him I was about to move out. For the past week or so, Rashard has been trying desperately to get me to move into the house he bought for us but he never said why. I don't understand how he can act the way he acts, then turn around and pursue me hard. When he pulls these disappearing acts, it makes me wonder who he's disappearing with. We never got a chance to talk about the coma situation, so I could ask questions to figure out if he was really in one or not. If not, I'd like to know why he would pretend to be in a coma.

"You gone come with me after we eat?" Amere asked, and I frowned my face up involuntarily. "To file the missing person report," he answered the question I was thinking. The brief conversation I just had with Rashard through text had me distracted.

"Yea," I answered, as I began to eat my sandwich.

After I finished eating, I went to my room and got dressed with Armani on my mind. She used to always insinuate that I should dress better. Oh, who am I kidding? Her ass use to straight up tell me I needed to dress better. I didn't really know what to wear without her or Candy here to help me, so I was going for the simple but cute look.

I slid into some black jeggins and cuffed the bottom of the pants legs all the way up to my calf. I threw on a red tank top shirt with my black and white Betty Boop cropped top shirt on top. I grabbed my red and black sandals and threw my hair in a tight ponytail with big hoop earrings. I took a step back and admired my reflection in the mirror.

I pulled out my phone and sent a text.

Tamia: just thinking bout you

Armani: funny how I was just about to text you! lol

Tamia: how r u

Armani: fine how about lunch?

Tamia: sure call me later with the place and time

Armani: alright

Our relationship has gotten drastically better. We don't talk as much as we use to and I'm perfectly fine with that. She also appears different, more mature than ever, and I think I can thank this new secret man in her life that she's always bragging about. You should have saw the look on her face when I asked her was it Rashard but shit, I just had to make sure we weren't about to do that again.

Speaking of that, Amere refuses to talk about it and he told me to stay as far away from her as heavenly possible. I thought that was very hypocritical for him to say, being as though I live with him.

I threw my phone in my purse and headed to the front of the house, so we could go. Amere was already dressed, so he was just waiting on me. "I'm going to meet you there because I have a lunch date with Mani," I said and watched anger wash over his face.

"I told you to stay away from her. Be careful," he said and hopped in his vehicle. I followed him down to the police station and waited with him until he finished all of the bullshit ass paperwork, along with getting questioned like he had done something to her. It seemed like everybody knew that Amiria turned out not to be his but luckily for him, he was hospitalized when she took off.

"I hope she's ok," I said, as we headed out of the precinct because even though I don't like her, I don't want anything to happen to her.

Michelle

I didn't know I had passed out until I woke up with the TV still on my back. I looked around and saw that Dre was now lying closer to me, as if he was coming to finish me off but passed out as well. I knew he was still alive because I could see his back rising and falling slowly. I used my arms to push my body up with the TV on me and buck it out the way. I didn't have time to play so once it toppled over, I grabbed my knife and crawled over to Dre's body.

I grabbed his head and pulled it back as far as it would go, so I could expose his neck completely. I took the knife and pressed it firmly against the left side of his neck, making sure I broke skin as I slid to the right side slicing his neck open. He woke up in a final attempt to save his life and grabbed at his throat.

I let his head go and sat on the couch as I waited for him to die. Once I was sure that he was dead, I grabbed my knives and walked into the kitchen to clean them off. I took one final look at Dre's dead body before I left out of the apartment.

When I got to the top of the staircase, I stopped for two reasons. The first reason is Twan was gone. After that shock wore off, I focused in on the rude neighbor that was now standing at the bottom of the staircase. She stared up at me with a shocked expression as her hand covered her mouth. I looked down and noticed that, once again, I was covered with blood.

I looked up at her and shook my head. "I don't have time for this shit!" I said out loud as I ran down the stairs. Too bad for me, she took off running and ran straight back to her car. She dropped the keys just as I made it to the bottom of the stairs. I tried to keep running but slipped on something wet. "Ah, fuck my life!" I screamed out once I realized it was Twan's blood.

I hopped up and ran as fast as I could to her car. I jumped on top of it as she backed out of her parking spot. This bitch sped off like I wasn't on her car. "Crazy bitch," I thought to myself as I began to punch the windshield of her car. I was punching it as hard as I could but my licks were doing nothing to it. She slammed on breaks and I flew off the top of her car and landed in rubbish.

"We're looking for Michelle Melton in connection with the murder of Andre..." I grabbed the remote and muted the television before the news anchor could finish her statement. I killed Dre six weeks ago and you would think they would just give it up already. Hell, it ain't like he was somebody important! He was an ain't shit ass nigga that was plotting to kill his best friend.

They got me holed up in the raggedly ass roach motel as I waited on the megabus to come to the station that's right across the street. I've shaved my head completely, so I wouldn't be easily recognized as I skipped town. It was only a $20 ride to Atlanta and I brought snacks, so I would never have to get off the bus. I peeked out the window just as the bus pulled up. I hauled ass all the way out of the room and to the bus stop and left everything behind but my wallet with my fake ID in it. I guess I'll catch Tamia later.

Rashard

I've been looking for Michelle's ass everywhere and I hadn't had any luck. I put a reward on her head for anyone who could bring her to me alive but it was like she had dropped off the face of the earth. That reason and that reason alone is why I was pressing so hard for Tamia to move into the house I bought her. I didn't want to have to worry about her getting hurt because I couldn't protect her. Hell, she won't even tell me where she is. I need her to move in today, so I can put all of my focus on finding Michelle before the police does. I saw her on the news, so I guess Lisa was right about her. Hell, Tiffany tried to tell me but I didn't even listen to her. I bet Michelle killed her too. Twan been missing in action for so long that I don't know if they killed him or if he's a part of it all.

I'm just glad Myra and Candy pulled through. Bo wasn't as lucky. He's in a coma and they're saying it doesn't look good for him. That shit is all his fault though. He should have teamed up with me instead of against me and maybe, just maybe, he wouldn't be in the hospital right now. My mama was on my ass about going to see him until I told her what happened to him and why. Hell, she stopped going to see him too.

Raphael's been blowing me up to come down to the club and see the new cage dancer he hired. Apparently, she's been raking in more dough than Candy was and those are big shoes to fill! Whoever she is, she's taking over, and it sounds like he better get a handle on her before she be gunning for his job. I'll get down there when I can though but right now, I need to make sure Chardae's ass is out of my house.

I hopped in my car and drove to Dead Man's Cove and picked up two smokers. I had $10 a piece to clean the house out for me, so I could put it up for rent. When we walked inside the house, I couldn't believe my eyes. This bitch wrecked my entire fucking crib, like she's Wreck It Ralph or something. I walked through the house and all of the flat screens were bent in and cracked from whatever she hit them with. I walked in the kitchen and she had broken every dish in that bitch! I went inside that baby's room and it was completely empty. Probably the only room that the smokers wouldn't have to clean.

"I'm going to give ya'll $20 apiece. Get started," I said, as I sat on the couch. I needed to make sure I dropped them off and made it to the new house to cook Tamia dinner before she got there.

Tamia

After we left the police station, we drove straight back home because Armani hadn't called me to meet her yet. I went straight to my room to start packing shit up to move, so Rashard wouldn't have to come here and help me. Hell, I didn't even want him to know I was ever staying here.

"You leaving?" Amere asked from the doorway.

"Yes. I'm moving in the house Rashard bought me," I said and heard him sigh dramatically. I turned around and gave him my undivided attention as I waited for him elaborate on his dramatics but he just stood there. "He's not going to be staying there with me. Everything's in my name and I just want my own space," I explained, although most of it was a lie.

Yes, my name is on the deed but so is Rashard's, so if he wanted to be there, he very well could. Amere just nodded his head and walked away and it couldn't have been at a better time because my phone chimed, indicating I had a text message.

Rashard: b home by 6 for dinner

I didn't reply but the smile that spread across my face could not be stopped. I packed faster than ever and began carrying my bags to my car. Rashard told me he had bought me a Benz truck and had I not been acting stupid, I'd have it now but instead, it's parked at my new house waiting on me to get some act right. I smiled brighter at the thought of him saying that, like he knew he had me at hello or some shit.

By the time I finished loading my car, Armani was ready for me to meet her for lunch, so I swung by the new house and carried my things inside. It felt like someone was watching me as I walked back to my car, so I quickened my pace and pulled off. I didn't even check to see if I saw anyone because my main concern was to get away from them.

Had I been inside I wouldn't have cared because Rashard has safe rooms and panic rooms all over the house! I don't know what he was thinking about when he had all of that installed.

Hell, I don't even know where he got the money to get all of this shit done.

I shook my head to rid myself of all of those thoughts as I drove to meet Armani.

Armani

Tamia and I pulled up at the restaurant at the same time and for the first time in a long time, I was happy to see her. Since Dave and I have been together, I've realized that I was just jealous of Tamia because it doesn't matter what life throws at her, she smiles and throws it right back. I was jealous of the strength that she has to overcome anything and the determination she has to be successful. I hated the fact that you could never look at her and tell when she was going through it. I use to say she thought she was better than me but now I see that it was me that thought she was better than me. Dave has showed me that nobody is better than me and that I can be successful too.

"Hey boo," I said, as I met her at the door and gave her a hug. I was excited because I had a surprise for her.

"Hey," she said, then opened the door for me to enter first. The host lead us to our table and she looked at me crazy when she saw the third seat.

"I have a surprise guest for you," I said then smiled. I noticed the look she gave me and it let me know that she still doesn't trust me. I don't blame her though because I wouldn't trust me either, but I've changed.

"Who?" she asked, just as my guest came strutting her extra sexy ass to our table. I nodded my head in her direction and Tamia turned to look at her. "Hey Candy!" she said all excited and what not, as she stood up to give her a whole hug. I felt the jealousy take over as I watched them embrace when she just gave me half a hug and a dry hey. I sucked my teeth as I waited for Candy to speak to me but she didn't.

They talked and caught up for ten minutes and 29 seconds, like I wasn't sitting at the table with them. I can't even tell you what they were saying because I had long since tuned them out after I spotted a familiar face as it entered the restaurant arm and arm with his wife! Yes, the wife he told me he left to be with me. I sat at the table stoned face, trying to calm myself down as pain and rage filled my soul.

I watched her laugh as he held her hands and stared into her eyes the same way he had been staring into mine. He didn't have to do me like that. We could have kept fucking with no strings attached, especially since Joe hasn't been around at all. I guess that was too much like right though. Why lead me on and play with my heart when my feelings weren't involved until you played on them? What did I ever do to deserve this? I was his shoulder to cry on about the bitch, for crying out loud.

I felt the hot tears sting my face as I stood up abruptly and knocked my chair over in the process. "Armani, what's wrong?" Tamia asked. I looked at her then back at Dave, who was now looking in my direction, along with everyone else in the restaurant but I didn't give a damn. I stormed over to their table pissed beyond measure.

"So, this how we doing it?" I asked him and completely ignored her.

"Who are you? Do we know each other?" he asked with a serious expression on his face. I reared back and slapped the shit out of him. When he looked back up at me, I could tell he was mad but so was I! I guess that made two of us.

"Sweetie, my husband may have fucked you and he may have paid you but don't get in your feelings about it. He does that from time to time. You aren't the first and you won't be the last. How much we owe you?" she asked with a slight smirk on her face.

I heard Tamia telling me to let it go as she tugged softly on my arm, but I was not about to leave this table. "You go be with your best friend," I said to her and gestured towards the door that Candy was walking out of. She huffed, rolled her eyes, and walked away. I should have known she wouldn't have my back.

"Sweetie, your husband been doing more than fucking me. He's been living with me these past couple of weeks. Now, ya'll owe me for about 18 years bitch, I'm pregnant!" I said, then grabbed both of their glasses, poured it on top of them, and left.

Tamia

I was so happy to see Candy and catch up with her and I had Armani to thank for that, but that bullshit she just pulled is not ok. I recognized that nigga as soon as I saw him as the sponsor that caught me watching them have sex. She should have known that he wasn't shit and left him alone, but she allowed her feelings to get involved; now, they're hurt.

I got a job I'd like to keep, so it's about that time that I cut her negative energy bringing ass completely off. I don't have time for that. I thought she was growing up and I thought that she was changing but she wasn't. She was still the same drama filled, trained to go Armani Wright from the coast. You got to want to be better and Armani just doesn't want to.

I shook my head as I followed Candy out the door and hopped in my car. I drove all the way to our new house with an uneasy feeling, but I didn't know why I was feeling that way. When I pulled up, Rashard was already there and came out to help me get my bags out of the car. I got the feeling that someone was watching me again as Rashard leaned over to kiss my forehead.

I looked around but I didn't see anyone, so I walked in the house behind Rashard. When I walked in, there were rose petals leading to a table for two. I walked right up to the table and took my seat. After Rashard put my bags in my room, he joined me. When I removed the lid from the tray, I couldn't do anything but laugh.

"What?" he asked with a smirk on his face. I looked at my plate with six chicken nuggets and French fries and couldn't help but laugh again.

"You tried," I said in between laughs.

"And put a smile on your face," he said, as he slid me the bottle of ketchup and cup of barbecue sauce. We dug in and ate the chicken nuggets. I was starving because I didn't eat when I was with Armani.

After we finished eating, he led me into the kitchen for wine and chocolate covered strawberries. We sipped wine and talked as we fed each other strawberries. Without notice, Rashard placed his soft lips against mine. He pulled me to the edge of the counter as we continued to kiss. I could feel his dick getting hard as the kiss deepened. My clit started to throb, so I slid closer and wrapped my legs around his waist.

I pulled him in as close as I could as I kissed him hungrily. This is something I'd be wanting since I met him and I was finally getting it. I pushed him away from me and pulled my shirt off. I undressed quickly as I watched him unbuckle his pants and drop them around his ankles. His boxers followed suit and his hard dick stood at attention. If I didn't know any better, I'd swear it winked at me.

He sat me back on the counter and dove head first in this pussy. I grinded against his face as he ate me out like it was his last meal. My body began to tremble as he slid me to the edge of the counter and continued to suck on my clit. He stood upright and kissed my lips, and I could taste my sweet juices on his tongue.

I felt his dick at the entrance as he slid in slowly. I moaned into his mouth as pain mixed with pleasure filled my body. He was grinding into me and I was going crazy. I threw my head back with my eyes closed and laid flat on the counter as he continued to give me long deep strokes. It didn't take long for me to have a body rocking orgasm.

When I opened my eyes, he was still going strong. He was winding his hips in a circular motion as he applied pressure to my clit with one hand and squeezed my nipple with the other hand. I sat up and wrapped my arms around his neck, and he lifted me off the counter. "Stand by the refrigerator," I said.

He moved to the refrigerator, still giving me strokes the whole way there. When we got there, I grabbed the top of it for leverage and rode him like crazy. We were both moaning out until we came together. He slid down to the floor, dick still inside of my throbbing pussy as we sat there, spent.

"I love you, Tamia," he said, as held on to me.

"So, this why you put me out?" I heard a female voice say.

Rashard

I couldn't believe my ears and when I opened my eyes and looked up, my jaw hit the floor. Chardae was standing in our kitchen on the other side of the counter with tears streaming down her face. I stood up and helped Tamia up and gave her her clothes to put on as I stood in front of her. "Answer me," Chardae said but I ignored her as I slipped my boxers on.

"Why is she in my house?" Tamia asked me and I shrugged my shoulders. "Leave," Tamia said to Chardae. "Both of you," she continued, as her knees buckled slightly.

"You put me out so you could move her in?" Chardae asked.

"Bitch, you weren't living here hoe! I put yo ass out because you set me up!" I snapped on her.

"You bought her a house too?" Tamia asked and I could feel myself sinking as Chardae nodded her head.

"This why," Chardae said and walked around the counter and raised her shirt to expose her pregnant belly. I looked back at Tamia but she didn't look all the way there.

"Tamia baby, I love you," I said, as I took a step towards her but she took one backwards. "I was gonna tell you when I found out if it was mine. This happened before us," I tried to explain but she didn't say anything. "Man Tamia, fuck this bitch; it's you that I want!" I yelled at her.

"Why? What makes her so much better? I thought you loved us," Chardae said and grabbed a knife off the counter.

"Bitch, don't be stupid. I told you I was gone be with her and that I didn't love you stop kidding yourself," I said, clearly aggravated.

"He's not worth-"

"SHUT UP!" Chardae yelled, cutting Tamia off. "He is worth it!" she said. "Why won't you be with me?" she asked with tears streaming down her cheeks.

"I told you I love her," I said, pissed off. I didn't give a fuck about that knife because I was gone punch her in her shit before she got a chance to stab me or Tamia.

"I had this baby so we could be a family. If you don't want a family, I don't want this baby," she said calmly, then raised the knife high in the air.

"NOOOO!" Tamia screamed and ran towards her but it was too late. I watched Chardae slam the knife in her stomach, drop to her knees, and fall forward.

Epilogue

Michelle gave her mission of killing Tamia a break with hopes of the police eventually leaving her alone, so she will be free to kill Tamia and claim Rashard as her man. She has faith that once Lisa finds out that Dre is dead, she won't snitch on her for killing Bo. She has no idea that Lisa is dead or that Bo is hanging on by a thread of faith.

Armani just found out she was pregnant the morning she decided to turn over a new leaf and help Tamia and Candy reconnect. She had hopes that she and Dave would raise their child together but now she doesn't know if she's going to keep it, considering he's still with his wife.

Tamia tried her hardest to keep Chardae alive until the ambulance showed up, while Rashard stood in the same spot in a state of shock. She succeeded. Unfortunately, the baby didn't make it. Now Rashard and Tamia has to figure out what they're going to do about their relationship.

****

"Sir, are you ready to tell us who you are?" the nurse asked and the patient shook his head. "Well, we are about to discharge you; do you have anyone that can come get you?" she asked and he shook his head. "Ok, well tomorrow you will be cleared to go," she said, then walked out of the room.

The nurse walked down to the nurse's station to talk to Dr. James about the patient they call "The miracle patient." He was shot in the back and had a collapsed lung from the gunshot wound. When the paramedics arrived, he had no heartbeat but they were able to resuscitate him. He was on a ventilator for almost two weeks before he could breathe on his own again. When they first pulled the tube from his mouth, he tried to talk but his throat was so dry.

The nurse gave him a cup of water, pen, and paper, and he wrote a message.

Tamia, I'm coming, was all it said but the nurse had no idea who Tamia was, and nobody came to visit him his entire time there. "He still won't tell us his name," the nurse said to the doctor in charge of his care. The doctor simply nodded his head and walked off, completely unaware of the danger he would be putting someone in by not getting authorities involved.

TRUE GLORY PUBLICATIONS

IF YOU WOULD LIKE TO BE A PART OF OUR TEAM, PLEASE SEND YOUR SUBMISSIONS BY EMAIL TO TRUEGLORYSPUBLICATIONS@GMAIL.COM. PLEASE INCLUDE A BRIEF BIO, A SYNOPSIS OF THE BOOK, AND THE FIRST THREE CHAPTERS. SUBMIT USING MICROSOFT WORD WITH FONT IN 11 TIMES NEW ROMAN.

Check Out Other Great Books From This Author

A Crazy Ghetto Love Story
A Crazy Ghetto Love Story 2

Addicted To Him

Addicted To Him II

Claim Code:
YRDT-ECYLSZ-BR6F
. Visit www.amazon.com/redeemgift.
2. Enter the Claim Code and click Apply to
Your Account.

CPSIA information can be obtained
at www.ICGtesting.com
Printed in the USA
LVOW10s1855020317
525948LV00011B/772/P